PROLOGUE

My heart feels like it's one beat away from bursting through my skin. It's so distracting that instead of listening to the men around me, I'm desperately trying to recall my training from the academy on what to do when someone goes into cardiac arrest.

I wipe my palms on the thigh of my jeans and try to take a deep breath.

I can't.

I feel like I'm suffocating.

Tears well in my eyes. Grinding my teeth, I push them away and pick a spot on the white plastic table to center myself. A muted coffee ring stain that looks like it's been there for a year.

Focus.

Slowly, the agents' voices begin to penetrate the haze of adrenaline coursing through my veins.

"...there's a plug-in over there," one says to the other.

"Okay, hang on."

Then, I hear the *click* of a tape recorder, followed by a second of silence while they stare at me.

The tension in the room is stifling.

And then, it begins.

My hands begin to tremble.

"Mrs. Velky." Agent Zeal speaks. "Do you understand why we just arrested you?"

A bead of sweat rolls down the side of my face.

"Cora Granger was found in her home, brutally beaten to death..." Zeal pauses, a strategy I have used countless times while interviewing suspects, "among her extensive injuries, the letter X had been carved into her skin. Our crime scene techs found DNA on her body and also at the scene of the crime. This DNA is a statistical match to yours. As you know, this is more than enough to give us probable cause to make an arrest... Do you care to explain why your DNA was on the victim's body and at the scene of the crime?"

My jaw clenches, my body trembling in fury at the uncontrollable tears gathering in my eyes. I cannot cry—*I will not.*

"Mrs. Velky," Agent Briggs says, "as I'm sure you are well aware, this is pretty much a slam dunk case. By denying legal counsel, and by your continued silence on the matter, you are basically admitting guilt. Do you understand that?"

"Yes."

"So are you admitting guilt?" Zeal asks. "Did you kill Cora Granger? Would you like to make a confession right now?"

"Yes."

A moment of shocked silence fills the room.

I look up, my teary eyes as cold as ice.

"I killed Cora Granger."

A MARRIAGE OF LIES

AMANDA MCKINNEY

Storm
PUBLISHING

Ebook ISBN: 978-1-80508-522-5
Paperback ISBN: 978-1-80508-524-9

Cover design: Lisa Horton
Cover images: Trevillion, Shutterstock

Published by Storm Publishing.
For further information, visit:
www.stormpublishing.co

ALSO BY AMANDA MCKINNEY

The Viper

Mad Women

The Raven's Wife

The Widow of Weeping Pines

The Lie Between Us

The Keeper's Closet

Berry Springs

The Woods

The Lake

The Storm

The Fog

The Creek

The Shadow

The Cave

Black Rose Mystery

Devil's Gold

Hatchet Hollow

Tomb's Tale

Evil Eye

Sinister Secrets

Standalones

Lethal Legacy

The Stone Secret

ONE

ROWAN

One week earlier

My stomach sinks at the sound of the garage door opening.

I sit taller against the pillow and glance at the clock—11:23 p.m.

Banjo whines and raises his head from the floor next to the bed. My side, where he always sleeps.

"It's okay, buddy, go back to sleep," I whisper, reaching down and scratching between his furry little ears.

The car engine turns off, the door slams closed.

I grab the television remote and unmute the evening news.

A rush of adrenaline sweeps through my body.

The front door opens, pulling a waft of cold, autumn air through the bedroom window. The door closes.

Footsteps.

All the things I had planned to say suddenly vanish into thin air. It's as if my brain short-circuits the second my husband steps into the doorway.

His stride breaks as our eyes meet. He didn't expect me to be awake.

The light from the television, the only light in the room, dances across a puffy, flushed face. He's drunk.

Again.

He shakes his head as if knowing what is about to come. Defeated, his shoulders slump as he crosses the room. He doesn't address me.

I do this to him. My mere existence exasperates my husband of fifteen years, his contempt for me so overwhelming at times that it renders him speechless.

Shepherd walks into the closet, flicks on the light. His long, black shadow stretches across the worn hardwood floor, disappearing under the bed. I watch as he unbuttons his shirt then rips it off dramatically like the Incredible Hulk. He's gearing up for a fight, and that's just fine with me. Stumbling, he tosses the shirt into the dirty clothes and I don't have to check to see that he missed. Shepherd is terrible at basketball, despite playing every Wednesday night for the last five years. The group of over-forties he meets at the local gym has been dubbed the "dad-bod squad." A cruel (hysterical) moniker that I pretend to be offended by.

The light clicks off, he disappears into the bathroom.

The anger inside me begins to dissolve. Forget the hours I've spent stewing while waiting for my husband to come home. The hours I've spent imagining every horrific scenario possible as to why he is so late, and then plotting how I would react to each one. Despite all that, the fact that he is now here makes everything else seem suddenly... well, less. Shepherd is safe. He is home.

He is *with me.*

I hear the whir of the toothbrush, the toilet flush. The light clicks off. I can smell the liquor on his breath as he slides between the cold sheets. Ignoring me, Shepherd rolls onto his side, taking half the blanket with him. This is a constant argument between us. My husband hogs the blanket (and most of the bed) while I freeze, clinging onto the edge of the mattress for dear life.

I yank back the blanket.

"What?" he snaps, the emotional pot boiling over.

I say nothing.

Shepherd sighs heavily, dramatically, the scent so pungent it would ignite the room if a match were lit. He aggressively adjusts the pillow underneath him. "Can you turn off the television?"

"Can you get a job?" I snap back and instantly regret it. Like my husband, I too have had too much to drink.

"What did you just say to me?" Shepherd rolls onto his back, and looks at me, his mouth agape. The tattoo he once got for me, a heart just below his collarbone, stares up at me, now faded and ugly.

"Where have you been tonight? It's after eleven o'clock. I've been worried sick. You didn't answer my texts. You told me—"

"I *told you* I went to play pool with the guys. The bar had a live band tonight. It was loud. Sorry."

The bar he is referring to is named Last Call. It's the only reputable bar in town. I know that it was busy tonight, just as I know that a band named Bjorn Again—a dreadful punk rock band comprised of the town doctor (newly divorced), the city librarian (his mistress), and an unorthodox Amish family of four —played there tonight. I know this because I checked the website. I also know this because I drove by—three times. My husband's truck was in the parking lot at eight o'clock, but *not* at nine-thirty. As of this moment, we have two hours unaccounted for.

Shepherd sits up, furious now—or defensive?

"You have one hell of a nerve telling me to get a job, Ro. You know I'm trying. And meanwhile you seem to have no trouble spending half my severance package to pay off your car and get a new pair of running shoes."

"*Our* car—it's our car. You drive the Explorer as much as I do." I turn toward him. "Shep, you were laid off *eight* months ago. You have had *four* job offers since then, and have rejected them all."

It isn't about the job. It never is. It's never about the words that come out of our mouths, is it? It's about the contempt we've built and buried deep inside our psyche. Years of all the things we should have said, but didn't. Little stones of disdain, guilt, blame, disappointment, slowly stacking one by one until the wall eventually breaks and releases in an outburst of disjointed half-thoughts and half-threats—none hitting the mark you intended, and all settling back into place, unresolved once again.

"How dare you," he spits. "Listen. If you want me to accept just any job, and be a miserable man, I'll do it. But I want to find a job that makes me *happy*, Ro. Because I sure as hell don't get any validation at home."

And there it is. The *actual* problem. I don't have sex with my husband enough, plain and simple. I don't shave my legs often enough. I don't trim enough. I don't "do myself up" enough. I don't wear the lingerie he buys for me. I don't present myself on a silver platter when my husband walks through the door, my legs spread, heels on, ball-gag in, lube in hand. And as much as I hate—*absolutely loathe*—to admit it, the guilt I feel for not indulging my husband is irrepressible. A wife should want to have sex with her husband.

Shouldn't she?

To be clear, I love my husband. I do. But things have changed, and this is where it gets tricky. Letting go feels impossible because Shepherd has become a part of me, like a vine over-taking a tree, wrapping, wrapping, wrapping until you are unsure where the tree begins and the vine ends. On a material level, we have a home, assets, retirement, stocks, all the things. On an emotional level, we have us, this unit we have become. I understand my husband on a deep, visceral level. I know what he is going to say before he says it, I know what he's thinking before he realizes it. I know every mole on his body, I know the little scar above his left eyebrow, I know that when he twirls his wedding band it means he is contemplating something. Shepherd is solely responsible for introducing me to love—literally, the feeling of it. Real, soulmate, written-in-the-stars, can't-live-without-you kind of love. The kind that flips you upside down, shakes you around, and obliterates everything you thought you knew about yourself. The kind of love that seems to change you on a molecular level. There is no life, none worth living at least, without this other person. It's both terrifying and thrilling at the same time.

But things have changed.

There was a time that Shepherd and I told each other everything. There were no secrets between us.

Until there were.

And even then—*even now*—I still love him.

But am I *in* love with him?

"I told you," I say, my resolve wavering. "I'm taking supplements that are supposed to increase my libido, and I made an appointment with my doctor to see if I'm going into early menopause. I'm doing everything I can. I am so sick of having this fight with you."

"*You're* sick of it?" He snorts. "You have got to be kidding me. You don't put any effort into our marriage but expect me to do everything I used to. God, Rowan, you..."

"I what?"

"Nothing."

"*What?*"

"You've totally let yourself go."

My stomach folds in on itself.

He continues, while I fight for breath. "You've totally

phoned in our marriage, but get mad at *me* for not doing enough."

My gaze flickers to the outline of my body under the covers. Yes, I've gained a bit of weight, and yes, I haven't updated the highlights in my brown hair in years, and yes, my once natural caramel skin tone has lost its golden luster.

As have I.

"Ro, all you do is work. You prioritize your goddamn job over anything else."

"Well I have to, don't I?" I snap. "I'm the only one with a job in this house."

Shepherd surges off the pillow, grabs a stale glass of water from the nightstand, and hurls it against the wall. Glass shatters. Water splashes across the television.

Banjo barks, jumps onto his hind legs and puts his paws on the bed. I gently lay my hand over the top of his head and subliminally tell him everything is okay.

Silence envelops us.

Finally, I speak, though it's barely a whisper. "Please. Just tell me, Shep. Where were you tonight?"

"No, Ro. *No.* I'm not doing this. I can't..." With a guttural groan, my husband pushes out of bed, cutting the bottom of his foot on a broken piece of glass.

He bellows in pain.

My pulse roars in my ears as I watch my husband hobble to the bathroom. Cursing, he turns on the faucet, grabs a tissue, and begins to pluck the glass from his foot.

My cell phone beeps from the nightstand, startling me.

I tap the screen, read the message, then rip off the covers. Carefully, I make my way to the closet with Banjo on my heels. I remove my satin pajama shirt—the one I ordered from Victoria's Secret a week before. The one my husband didn't notice. I wrestle into a beige sweater and a pair of faded jeans. Boring clothes for boring me who never "does herself up." Plucking the hair-tie off my wrist, I tie my long, brown hair into a ponytail. I realize my sneakers are in the bathroom, so unfortunately, I have to pass my husband to get them.

Shepherd stops and turns when he realizes I'm dressed. Blood drips from his fingertips.

"Where the hell are you going?"

"To work," I say.

TWO

ROWAN

Arrival time three minutes, the GPS announces from the dashboard.

I click on the high beams. The fluorescent light shimmers against the asphalt, wet from a recent rain. Mounds of brown, brittle leaves crowd the ditches. A crescent moon hangs low in the sky, surrounded by a million stars.

It's a cool, clear autumn night, a prelude to what is predicted to be a rough winter ahead.

There are no streetlights in this neighborhood. Instead, ornate lampposts line the newly paved two-lane road, their orange orbs encircling the copse of trees that surrounds each one. Beyond the light, miles and miles of forest. My windows are down and I can just barely hear the lake lapping against the shore in the distance.

Unlike the secluded neighborhood I live in, these woods are manicured, resembling a park. The residents here have plenty of money to pay for year-round landscaping.

I try to remember the last time I responded to a call on this side of town. I can't.

Blackbird Cove is a small town ninety minutes north of

Houston, located on the edge of the Sam Houston National Forest, right outside of Lake Conroe. I was born and raised here, back when tractors clogged the roads, when the height of entertainment was starting a bonfire in the middle of the woods, and when pride was defined by our lack of anything chain-store. Now, however, the town has doubled in size due to an influx of Houston retirees seeking solace from the city. Amenities include golf courses, guided horseback trails, club houses, and twenty-four-hour spas.

There are two types of people in Blackbird Cove: One, hardworking blue-collar southerners stuck in a perpetual time-warp. And two, retired rich people.

The neighborhood I have been called to tonight is called Mirror Lakes—the unofficial name given to the area of town where "the money" settled.

My interest is already piqued.

I pass a grandiose two-story brick home with nightlights centered in every window. The next house is hidden by a veil of trees but appears to be another brick monstrosity.

I slow as I near the next home marked by a gold mailbox and a long, paved driveway.

"Your destination is on the right," the GPS announces.

I click the turn signal. My department-issued Impala squeaks and groans over the dip that leads into the driveway, reminding me to get the front end aligned.

Dozens of small pathway lights illuminate a windy path through tall, mature trees that eventually leads to a large stone mansion. Four vehicles crowd the circle drive: one police car, one unmarked, an ambulance, and a jacked-up gunmetal-gray Chevy that I recognize instantly.

The house is the biggest on the block, tall and fat, like a medieval castle. Twin lions flank an impressive arched entryway with a port cochere. Every single light is on.

I roll to a stop behind the Chevy, crack the windows, and

turn off the engine. A gust of cold night air whips past me as I dip out of the car. I chide myself for not grabbing a coat on the way out. I always forget a coat.

I open the rear door.

"I'll be back, buddy-boo." Ruffling Banjo's ears, I pull the backpack from the floorboard. My best friend licks my wrist then torments me with a whine before I close the door. I reach into the side pocket of my pack and toss him a dog treat.

"Just a bit, then I'll take you out," I promise into the cracked window.

After looping the pack over my shoulder, I weave through the vehicles.

Outside the home, a uniformed police officer is interviewing an elderly man in a gray terry cloth robe. They are standing under a gaudy six-foot chandelier hanging over the front entry of the home. The man's hair is snow white, but his skin is tanned, giving him an almost cartoonish appearance. Flannel cotton pants cover his legs, leather slippers over his feet.

The witness.

THREE

ROWAN

"Detective Velky." The officer nods as I approach. I recognize him as Nick Anderson, a rookie cop. He hands me the crime-scene sign-in log and makes the introduction. "Mr. Hoyt, this is Detective Rowan Velky."

The man inhales deeply, and turns to me. Relieved, I think, and also shaken. Sun-spotted, gnarled hands tremble at his side. His eyes, however, are blue as water and crystal clear.

I sign the log and hand the clipboard back to Anderson, my focus locked on the witness. "Mr. Hoyt, can I get you some water? Anything?"

"No. I'm fine," His voice carries the wear and tear of his age.

"I was just taking his statement," Anderson explains.

I nod. "Mr. Hoyt, I'm going to chat with my partner inside for a moment. Do you mind if I speak with you after Officer Anderson finishes his report?"

"Of course. Please."

"Thank you."

I nod to Anderson—*continue*.

Muffled voices float from open windows as I step to the

front door. After slipping a pair of blue booties over my sneakers and black nitrile gloves over my hands, I enter the home.

My partner, Detective Kellan Palmer, nods at me from the far end of the foyer. He is speaking with another officer, this one I don't recognize. I take a second to look around.

Despite the castle-like exterior of the home, the inside is surprisingly modern. Everything is white. Gleaming black and white checkered floors stretch to a double grand staircase that leads to a catwalk that extends the length of the foyer. Above my head, another massive chandelier. To my left is a large sitting room—white couches, white chairs, white drapery. To my right, sweeping windows showcase a garden outside, illuminated by an outdoor security light.

Kellan dismisses the officer and meets me under the chandelier.

"Nice place," I mutter.

"You should see the pool out back. It's got a grotto."

"Well hold onto your swim-shorts for a bit."

Ignoring the quip, Kellan frowns, looking me over in the way he does every time he sees me. Assessing, assessing. Judging.

"I was just coming outside to call you," he says.

"Why?"

"You were taking an unusually long time to get here and you didn't respond to my last text."

"I must've missed it," I say, my focus sweeping the interior of the home.

"Listen, I know it's your day off. I almost didn't call, but I knew you would've wanted me to. But I can handle this if you need to go. I've got your back, Rowan, you know that."

My brow cocks. "I've got my own back, thank you. But, no, I'm glad you called. I'm good."

A beat passes between us.

"You okay?" He presses.

"Yeah. Why?"

"You look... stressed or something."

"Thanks a lot." *You, on the other hand, look as handsome as always.*

A former marine, Detective Kellan Palmer joined BCPD three years earlier, after leaving the military. His unwavering commitment to the job got him promoted to detective in record-time, becoming the second-ever in Blackbird Cove. Me being the first. Kellan has been assigned as my partner, to shadow me while I train him until he's ready to be on his own. If I'm being honest, I haven't minded having Kellan on my heels for the last few months. The man is pure eye candy—tall, handsome, and built like an ox. He carries an air of competence that makes women melt. I know this because when he first moved to town, you couldn't go anywhere without hearing women swooning over him. As if that weren't enough, his reputation precedes him. While in the military, Kellan was awarded the Navy Cross, one of the most distinguished decorations the military offers. His work ethic is second to none. He is always the first on the job and the last to leave. Also, he's funny. Kellan Palmer would be perfect, I muse, if not for the fact that he isn't a dog person.

Kellan is twenty-nine years old and at his physical and mental prime. I am forty-one years old and peri-menopausal.

I smooth my sweater, a rush of insecurity coming over me. No makeup, messy ponytail, jeans that are a bit too snug (didn't used to be), and worn running shoes. I feel like this a lot lately, insecure.

"So where is she?" I ask, forcing aside the insecurity. "She" being the dead body that the witness, Mr. Hoyt, found.

"Upstairs in the master."

I tilt my head, noticing the shift in his tone. "What?"

"She's... I didn't think things like this happened around Blackbird Cove."

"Murder happens everywhere."

"Not like this."

Kellan fills me in as we climb the curved staircase.

"The station got a call about ten-thirty from the neighbor, Mr. Hoyt, after he discovered the body. He says he became suspicious when he hadn't seen the homeowner, Alyssa Kaing, leave in over two days. He says he became officially concerned after the lights had been on inside the home for two straight days now."

"Kaing, that's an interesting last name."

"It's Japanese. She took her husband's name."

We step onto the second-floor landing. White and gray marble runs under arched doorways and hallways. Recessed lighting gives the walls a golden glow. The word *opulence* runs through my head. Someone in this home has lots of money and likes to show it off.

Kellan continues, "Hoyt said it was suspicious because Alyssa and her husband always turn the lights off at nighttime— as most people do. I get the vibe he's one of those neighborhood watchers. Anyway, about an hour ago, he got worried enough that he decided to come over and check on her. When no one answered, he used his key to enter the home."

"He has a key to the home?"

Kellan nods. "Apparently, Alyssa gave it to him two weeks ago. They're friendly, according to Mr. Hoyt, meet for wine or afternoon tea sometimes. They both like to garden and struck up a friendship that way. Hoyt says Alyssa gave him a key in case there was ever an emergency."

I frown.

"Yeah, exactly," Kellan's eyes narrow. "I thought that was kind of odd too, considering two weeks later, there appears to be one hell of an emergency—she winds up dead."

"Is there a Mrs. Hoyt?"

"No. He's a widower, so he says."

"You don't believe him?" I ask.

"Didn't say that."

"When someone says, 'so he says,' it usually means they are suspicious of whatever was said."

"Ah. So, like, Detective Velky is okay... *so she says*."

I roll my eyes but inwardly wince. I hate my current mood, but more than that I hate that I am unable to conceal it.

Before we reach the master bedroom, pops of light bounce off the walls, accompanied by the *click, click, click* of the crime scene investigator's camera.

We step to the doorway. The room is lit up like a stage, the lamps and overhead lights on full-blast. Wearing a white jump-suit and hairnet, the medical examiner is on her knees, next to the body. On the floor next to her sits a medical bag, tweezers, scalpel, multiple plastic baggies, some of which contain bloody pieces of hair or skin that she has already removed from the body.

At the center of the scene is a woman lying in the middle of a white shag carpet, in front of a four-poster king-size bed.

I am taken aback by the brutality before me. Kellan did not prepare me for this.

FOUR

ROWAN

The victim is a young woman—I guess somewhere in her early thirties—with long blonde hair. She's tan and noticeably fit. Tattoos cover both her arms. She's wearing a white ribbed tank top stained with droplets of blood. The letter X has been carved across each of the woman's eyes. The gaping incisions extend from above her eyebrow to her nose, in a precise crisscross. Rivers of dried blood run down her pale cheeks like crimson tears. She's naked from the waist down.

The smell is atrocious.

I step deeper into the room, careful to stay out of the way of the crime-scene tech.

Darcy Banks, the overworked, underpaid medical examiner, glances at me as I approach. Her eyes are red and her face is pale. From being ripped away from the comfort of her bed, or from the brutality of the crime, I'm not sure. Darcy has been the county medical examiner since I can remember. Once a vibrant, auburn-haired country-girl who could drink any man under the table, now a fully-gray loner with a coldness behind her eyes that reflect decades of dissecting murder.

We stare at each other for a moment, a moment of awe

between two women. Astonishment that we are both in the presence of such evil—once again.

I blink, turn to Kellan who is staring down at the body with his hands in his pockets. He, too, is a little pale.

I want to scold him for not giving me the proper heads up before walking in on something like this. But instead, I return my focus to Darcy.

"Any sign of vaginal or anal penetration?" I ask, a knot catching my throat.

"No, I don't think she was raped, but I'll know more when I get her into the lab. But there doesn't appear to be any vaginal ripping or bruising to suggest it."

It's then that I notice the victim's neck is mottled with purple bruises.

"Was she strangled?"

Darcy nods. "I think so, yes. The contusions suggest manual strangulation. Not a string or ligature, but I'll verify that once in the lab."

"Do you think that's the cause of death?"

"My gut says yes, but I can't be certain yet."

"Understood. How long do you think she's been dead?"

"Two days."

That explains the smell.

Turning to Kellan I say, "That corroborates with the witness's story that the lights have been on for two days. She must have been killed sometime before she went to bed, and therefore the lights were never turned off."

"That would have been Monday evening," Kellan confirms.

"Where is the husband?" I ask, my mind beginning to spin.

"According to the travel itinerary I found on the kitchen table, he's in Japan for work," Kellan says. "He works at a tech startup company. I saw his business cards in an office down the hall."

"We need to verify that he's out of the country."

Kellan nods.

"It doesn't seem there was much of a struggle," I say, glancing around the room. Everything appears to be in place. Nothing tipped over, broken, or overturned. Nothing to suggest that there was a scuffle.

"Whoever did this could've overpowered her," Kellan adds. "She's pretty small."

"Or she knew whoever it was, and that person took her by surprise. Have you checked the house for any signs of a break-in, or a point of entry?"

"Not yet."

"I'll do that." I shift my attention to the medical examiner. "How much longer do you need with her?"

"Give me about twenty minutes, then I'll bag her up and take her to the lab."

"How soon do you think you can get the autopsy done?"

Darcy shoots me a look, one I've seen many times before, and one that I am certain I will see many times again. Darcy is the only medical examiner in the county, and therefore is grossly overworked and backlogged. She receives a constant flow of rush requests—like I am asking of her now.

She says, "I have several ahead of her, but I'll push her up the list."

"Thank you." I refocus on Kellan. "Have you found the woman's cell phone?"

"Yep. In the bathroom. It's already bagged up and tagged as evidence."

"Good. Her purse?"

"Downstairs, in the kitchen."

"Anything interesting inside it?"

"No."

I kneel down to get a better view of the woman's tattoos.

"Look at this one," Darcy points, "over here."

I shimmy closer to the victim's torso, avoiding the dried,

stinking bodily fluids that have seeped out of her body over the last forty-eight hours. Embedded in a collage of roses is the letter A, enclosed in a circle.

"The anarchy symbol."

Darcy nods. "And now look at the crease in her elbow."

I squint, lean closer. Kellan is now hovering over my back, covering his nose. I count at least a dozen tiny dots speckled over the victim's median cubital vein.

My brow cocks. "Needle scars?"

"I think so," Darcy confirms. "I've seen my fair share of needle marks and those are pretty spot-on. I'll do a toxicology scan on her first thing, see if I can rush that, too. That'll tell us if she had any drugs in her system at the time of death."

"Do you think this was drug-related?"

"In this community, I'd be surprised."

"They don't look fresh," I observe.

"I agree, and the anarchy tattoo looks old as well; kind of like she tried to cover it up with the flowers."

Rehabilitated. Or found God, maybe.

I stand up, consider the plush master bedroom. Already I'm getting the sick sense that something isn't adding up. How did this young, anarchy-tattooed woman, with a (possibly) sordid past, end up married to a tech executive and living in a multi-million-dollar home?

I turn to Kellan. "I'm going to go downstairs and talk to the witness, then check the house for signs of a break-in. Can you get Evelyn on the phone? I want a team meeting scheduled for first thing in the morning."

Evelyn is our admin officer, but I like to call her our every-thing officer. She's a fifty-one-year-old widow—married to a cop who lost his life in the line duty—whose role is to support ongoing criminal cases within the county. Another overworked, underpaid workhorse who has dedicated her life to help rid the world of evil.

Kellan grabs my arm as I turn. I spin around, my gaze darting to the others in the room.

He leans in. He smells like fresh soap. "I've got this if you need to go home and rest," he whispers.

I pull away my arm, run my sweaty palms over the thigh of my jeans. "No. I'm good." Before he can protest, I turn and stride out of the room.

My chest feels tight as I make my way down the hall. My stomach is queasy. I feel sweat beading underneath my sweater. I drag in a deep inhale and remind myself of what my therapist advised I do in panic-inducing situations. Focus on the now, on what is immediately in front of me, in *this* moment. Sight, touch, hear, smell, and taste.

Slowly, I make my way down the staircase, mentally cataloging everything I see while looking for anything out of place. I come up with nothing because the home is immaculate. I make a mental note to find out who does the housekeeping—just a hunch that the victim, Alyssa, doesn't scrub toilets.

I step onto the first floor as Officer Anderson is crossing the foyer.

"I was just coming to get you," he says. "Are you ready to talk to the witness?"

No. "...Yes."

FIVE

ROWAN

"Mr. Hoyt, thank you so much for waiting."

Amos Hoyt shakily pushes off the brick retaining wall where he's been sitting. He's shivering and his eyes are heavier than they were thirty minutes ago. The adrenaline rush from seeing a dead body is crashing. Rookie Anderson shouldn't have left him alone. I make a mental note to tell him that next time I see him.

"Would you like to go inside to chat," I ask, "or perhaps to your house if that would be more comfortable? Next door, correct?"

"My house, yes," Hoyt says quickly, apparently eager to put distance between him and the crime scene.

"Great. Lead the way."

We fall into step together. I notice a slight limp in Hoyt's right leg, though it doesn't seem to slow him down. In fact, he moves quicker than I anticipated. A gust of uncomfortably cold wind whips between us, sending my hair spiraling around my face. I glance at my car as we pass, at Banjo's dark silhouette in the back seat.

I see you buddy; I'll be back soon.

Hoyt leads us across the driveway and through the copse of trees that serve as a natural barrier between the Kaings' property and his. My eyes take a moment to adjust to the darkness. Hoyt, however, crosses the wooded terrain as if he's done it a million times. I realize we're walking on a worn footpath that connects the two homes. I take note of this.

"Do you visit Alyssa Kaing often?"

"No—well, yes." I have to pick up my pace to keep up with him. "I introduced myself to Alyssa and her husband Zach when they moved in a year or so ago. Shortly after, Alyssa and I kept running into each other at the edge of our back yards. We both like to garden—me fruits and vegetables, her flowers and plants, and we struck up a friendship."

A lonely widower looking for companionship, it would seem. But again, I've learned to assume nothing.

"Is there a Mrs. Hoyt?" I ask, though I know the answer.

"She passed away three years ago. Breast cancer."

"I'm sorry."

He nods.

We cross over into his front yard. Hoyt's home resembles the others on the street, brick and big.

"You have a beautiful place."

"Thank you."

We step onto the front porch, under a bright security light. Unlike the Kaings' home, this one is dark, void of interior light. Hoyt flicks on an entry light as we step inside. The musty scent of an underused, aged space clings to the air. The home doesn't share the grandeur of the Kaings'. It is at least thirty years past its prime and badly in need of renovations. The hardwood floors are faded and scratched, the varnish completely worn away. Dated wallpaper covers the walls. Thin, thread-worn carpet lines the rooms.

I am led down a narrow, dark hallway. Hoyt turns on lights as we go. My gaze shifts from room to room, seeking a line of sight to the Kaings' home, but the downstairs view is blocked by the trees.

The kitchen is large but simple. Only the necessities. The countertops are bare save for a microwave that reminds me of the one I had in college, and a toaster that I'm sure was once silver. An antique hutch sits caddy-corner, displaying a folded American flag and multiple medals.

"Were you in the military?"

"Marines. Can I get you something to drink?"

"Water. Thank you for your service."

I think of Kellan who was also a marine.

Hoyt doesn't elaborate, as I have found is common with most former soldiers. They are a humble breed.

He pulls a spotted drinking glass from the cabinet and fills it with tap water. I notice the sunspots and scabs that speckle his arthritic hands.

He sets the glass on the kitchen table, in front of me.

Neither of us sit, so I get to the point.

"Would you mind repeating to me what led you to go to the Kaings' house tonight?"

I listen as Hoyt recites the exact story Kellan told me when I arrived at the scene—the old man became worried after the lights on the house had not been turned off in over two days, and he had not seen the homeowners a single time.

"Did you try reaching out to Alyssa before going over to her house?"

"Yes. I called her cell phone three, maybe four times. No answer."

I make a mental note that Hoyt has Alyssa's cell phone number, in addition to a key to the home. This implies that at some point Alyssa felt comfortable enough to give her neighbor her personal phone number and a house key. Both intimate, personal things.

"When did you start calling her cell phone?"

"I called yesterday morning and then again this morning." He scratches his head. "And I think again this afternoon. When I laid down in bed tonight, I couldn't sleep. I knew something was wrong. So, finally, I just went over there."

"Did you go straight to the front door?"

"Yes, I rang the doorbell, then knocked a few times."

"Is this when you used your key to enter the house?"

"Not at that point. I went around back. Knocked on the back door. When there was no answer, I used the key."

"The key works for both doors? Or did she specifically give you a key to the back door?"

"I don't know. I just inserted it and it worked."

"The back yard is gated. Was the gate locked as well?"

"No. In fact, I think it was unlatched."

Interesting.

"Did you hear anything when you walked inside?"

"No," Hoyt crosses his arms over his chest and I spy a large tattoo of an anchor on his bicep. "The opposite, actually. I remember thinking how quiet it was."

"No television? Music?"

"No. I checked the kitchen first, then the den and the sunroom—as she likes to call it—and then went upstairs. That's when I found her. I called 911 immediately."

"Did you stay in the room after you called?"

"No. I went downstairs and waited on the front porch. I've seen enough crime shows to know that I shouldn't touch anything."

"Good job. Did you touch her at all? Maybe to check for a pulse?"

"No. The smell was enough to let me know she was dead."

"Understood. Mr. Hoyt, can you tell me about Mr. Kaing?"

Hoyt shifts his weight and for the first time, seems to hesitate. "I really don't know him that well. I've only met him twice, I think. He was nice enough, polite. He's not really a talker.

Didn't seem to have an interest in getting to know me, which is just fine."

"You only met him twice?"

"Yes, he works a lot. Leaves the house early in the morning and doesn't get home until late. Travels constantly." He pauses and I get the sense he's omitting something.

"What did Alyssa say about him, if anything?" I ask.

"Not much. We didn't really talk about him." His gaze drops to the floor.

"Do they have kids?"

"No... although..." He clears his throat.

I lean forward, placing my palms on the table. "Mr. Hoyt, now is not the time to hold anything back. Please tell me what you know."

"I think... I know that Alyssa was having trouble getting pregnant. I think he wants kids, and they've been trying for a while. I only know this because I offered her wine one day and she said she couldn't and then blurted out the story. I think it bothered her."

"What did?"

"The whole not being able to get pregnant thing."

He's starting to clam up—perhaps uncomfortable with gossip, or uncomfortable with me realizing how close he and the victim were.

A moment of silence stretches between us, my instincts tingling.

"Can I call you Amos?"

"Yes, of course."

"Amos, Alyssa Kaing gave you a key to her home, her cell phone number, and apparently confided in you about some heavy things."

"She's lonely."

"Lonely people don't just hand out their house keys."

He doesn't respond.

"May I ask if you two had an intimate relationship?"

"N... no." His eyes pop open. "No. No, nothing like that."

When I don't respond, he continues. "I promise, I would never. She's, God, how much younger than me? Too young. No, I would never."

"Okay. Sorry, I had to ask. What about Mr. Kaing? Was he jealous of your friendship with his wife?"

My question about intimacy has stunned him. He takes a second to compose himself. "Not that I'm aware of. Listen, Detective, I understand your job, but you are going way off track here."

"I understand, and I apologize for the uncomfortable questions. I'm just trying to get every detail I can."

He swallows deeply. "I understand."

"Thank you. This key... the fact that she gave it to you in case of an emergency. Tell me more about this."

"It happened about two weeks ago."

"Can you remember exactly when? The exact day?"

"No. But she came to my house—she never does that, so it surprised me. She gave me the key and said that it would make her feel comfortable for someone else to have access to the home in the event of an emergency."

"And what do you think she meant by 'emergency'?"

"I don't know, but those were her words exactly. I didn't think much of it because it seemed kind of normal to me... Call me old-fashioned but I feel like it's normal to give a trusted neighbor a key, maybe to check the house during a vacation, or turn off a forgotten oven, things like that. I didn't think much about it to be honest with you."

Amos Hoyt is lying.

"Would you mind showing me the view you have of the home?"

He frowns.

"You said the same lights have been on for forty-eight hours.

I'm curious where in this house you have a clear shot of the Kaings' windows."

"Oh," he nods. "Up in my bedroom."

I follow him upstairs to the master bedroom, which is much like the rest of the home. Dated, with antique furniture badly in need of polish, peeling wallpaper, and a musty scent.

Hoyt gestures to a double glass door that leads to a small deck. Sure enough, there is a break in the trees that allows for a full view of most of the Kaing home.

"Mind if I step outside?"

"Of course."

I slide open the door and step onto the small balcony. Hoyt follows.

"I sit out here a lot," he says, his body backlit by the porch light, his craggy face darkened by shadows.

I say nothing, shifting my focus to my hearing. I can hear the waves of the lake in the distance, and just barely, I can hear the voices of the officers speaking outside of the Kaing home.

"Did Alyssa and Zach ever have arguments that you might've heard while sitting out here?"

He pauses—and I am now certain he's leaving out something.

"Everyone argues," he says.

"Did they?"

"Yes, a few times, but nothing alarming."

"Was there yelling?"

"Raised voices. I wouldn't call it yelling."

"How many times have you heard raised voices?"

"A few. Not many."

"When was the last time?"

"A couple of weeks ago."

"So right around the time she gave you the key?"

He doesn't respond, and appears to take a second to digest the implication.

"Alright, well, thank you very much, Amos. Would it be okay if I visit again, or call you, if I have any other questions?"

"Anytime. I'll walk you out."

As I turn to follow Hoyt into the house, I notice three pairs of binoculars sitting on the coffee table, next to a half-burned marijuana joint.

SIX

ROWAN

"How is she?"

I lean back against the headrest and blow out a breath. Opening one eye, I peer at the clock glowing from the dashboard—3:04 a.m.

It's been a long night.

"She didn't recognize me this morning," I mutter.

Kellan releases a long exhale. "That must have been hard." His hand slips over mine, resting on the console between us. As if feeling the sudden shift in the air, Banjo drops his jaw on my shoulder, his furry little head squeezed between the driver's seat and driver's window. I reach back, give him a scratch behind the ears.

"Talk to me," Kellan says, gently caressing his thumb along the back of my hand. "What happened?"

"She was awake when I got up this morning, which was unusual."

"What time was that?"

"Five-thirty." I roll down the window, suddenly needing air. "She usually sleeps until past eight. I walked into the kitchen and she was sitting, fully dressed, at the kitchen table, just staring at the wall. The overhead lights were off. Her hands were folded on her lap, her posture was rigid... I don't know, like she was in a waiting room or something."

"Like she *thought* she was in a waiting room?"

"Exactly. It startled me, seeing her. I turned on the light and she just stared at me..." A knot grabs my throat. I'm tired, hungry, angry, but wound up like a spindle. I should be home. I should be sliding into bed next to my husband. I should be asleep. Instead, I am sitting in my car with my partner, in the middle of the woods, in the middle of the night.

"She was totally dead behind the eyes; do you know what I mean? Vacant... void of life—void of anything."

Kellan nods, but says nothing. He's good at that. Listening when he should, speaking when he should. A rare quality in a man.

I watch a bat zip past the windshield, a tiny flash of black against the rising moon in the distance. I startle, a jolt of fear slicing through my body. Thankfully Banjo doesn't notice the tiny little devil-creature.

I continue. "I said, 'Aunt Jenny, you scared me. What are you doing?' And she frowned as if she were confused. That's when I realized she didn't recognize me."

Bored with me now, Banjo slips onto the floorboard, rests his head on the console, requesting a scratch from Kellan.

"What did you do?" Kellan asks, scratching between Banjo's ears.

"I recalled what her doctor told me to do—to avoid asking if she knows who I am, and instead, to revert to routine and act like everything is normal. I'm supposed to understand that this can be very stressful for her, too, not recognizing the person she's with." I take a deep breath. "So, I tried to be as calm and cool as possible. I made breakfast, casually talking about the weather, current events, family, anything I could think of to spark her memory."

Kellan shakes his head then moves to scratch Banjo's other ear.

"She watched me closely the entire time and I could tell her mind was racing. About an hour later, she seemed to calm and she called me by my name."

"Did you report it?"

"Yes, to April, the nurse that picks her up every morning and takes her to the nursing home for the day. She's new. Took Inez's place."

"And what did April say?"

"That I did good, did what I was supposed to do, and that she'd have the doctor call me about adjusting Jenny's medication, which he did, and we're increasing her dosage."

"Good. How was Aunt Jenny when they dropped her off this afternoon?"

"Her normal, happy self." I snort. "She told me my hair was too dark."

Kellan grins. "She tells you that every day."

"She sure does." I grab a strand that had escaped the ponytail and examine the end. My hair was blonde as a child, which is what I assume my aunt is remembering. "Anyway, she went to sleep at seven and then I left at eleven-thirty tonight to respond to the Kaing homicide. I'm hoping she's still asleep; I'm sure she is. She usually sleeps through the night."

Yes, I've omitted much from this update, namely how my husband came home drunk, how he thinks I'm a dried-up hag, how I think he's having an affair, and also that he shattered a glass against the wall.

"Shepherd is there now, yes? If she needs something?" Kellan asks, reading my thoughts.

I nod. Sometimes I think I have a visible reaction when thinking about my husband. I'm not surprised Kellan has picked up on it.

A moment stretches between us.

"You know," he says, "I was doing some research today and I also called a buddy of mine whose mom went through Alzheimer's. There's a facility in Dallas that he took her to. Supposed to be amazing. And, according to him, they have flexible payment plan options that are unmatched anywhere in the state."

I close my eyes and sigh. Money. Sometimes it feels like the entire world revolves around it.

My eighty-one-year-old aunt, Jennifer Willmont, my only living relative, was diagnosed with Alzheimer's disease seven months ago. When I realized her former husband and her only living child weren't giving her the care she needed, I drove 270 miles to Dallas, where I packed her up, and moved her into our home in Blackbird Cove. I had my husband's blessing at the time, but based on the thick air of tension that has settled in the house, I don't think I do anymore.

Without meeting Kellan's gaze, I loop my finger around his. "Thank you for listening."

As Banjo snores in the backseat, we stare into the murky darkness ahead. Straight ahead, a steep, craggy cliff glows in the moonlight. Two weathered picnic tables sit haphazardly at the base of it, covered in graffiti. Dueling oak trees flank the space, each a different shade of orange. We've named them Laverne and Shirley. Laverne is my favorite of the two. She's turned a glorious shade of yellow-orange. Almost golden. Below them, a blanket of brown, brittle leaves cover the ground.

Kellan leans over. "It's okay to get help for her, Rowan. Twenty-four-hour professional care can be a blessing at this point."

"I don't need a break, Kellan." I pull my hand away and scrub my palms over my face. Kellan is right. I know he is, but I'm not ready to let her go.

Not yet.

SEVEN

ROWAN

Kellan and I first came to "The Cliff" while working a lead on one of our first cases together. Once a park, now shut down due to budget cuts, the small clearing sits under a cliff on the outskirts of town. Families used to hike up from the lake to picnic under the soaring oaks, but now it's just leaves and rocks. I remember Kellan commenting how beautiful it is. Funny, I'd never noticed. That's the thing about Kellan. He shows me things. Not physically, but cerebrally. He makes me see things in a different light, notice things that I never have before. Appreciate them. After that first case, we met again on a warm spring day for a working lunch. I was the one who suggested the place. Two lunches turned into three, then a meeting after work. Somewhere in there, The Cliff became "our" place. Sometimes with coffee, sometimes with wine, sometimes with a six-pack of cheap beer.

We've spent hours at a time here, just the two of us, talking about the silliest things. What we would do if we won the lottery; if alien life exists; why he never wears cologne; why I always wear my hair in a ponytail; our celebrity crushes; our spirit animals, and our most embarrassing moments (his involves a feral fox, a bottle of silly string, the end of a broomstick, and seven stitches in a very private place). We've engaged in several heated debates, analyzing in great detail if *Die Hard* is a Christmas Movie (it's *NOT*), if a hotdog is a sandwich, and finally, whether Tony died in the final episode of the Sopranos (this last one went on for a while).

We've even discussed religion and politics.

In a weird way, Kellan has become my best friend. Someone I can always count on to have my back, to listen, and to make me laugh.

With Shepherd, more often than not, I feel like a mother to him. With Kellan, I feel like a partner.

To be honest, I'm not sure what is happening here. But I do know that I have not stopped it. That I have indirectly accepted this immoral behavior by allowing it to continue. Our relationship has been alarmingly easy for me to justify. Then again, it's easy to justify things that make us feel good, isn't it? Before Kellan, every day felt like a fight. Between me and my husband, me and my job, me and my aunt's dying brain, between me and myself. Kellan's entry into my life has changed all that.

Maybe the former marine is nothing more than a distraction. Or maybe it's the simple fact that Kellan makes me happy. He makes me feel pretty and respected. He listens to me—he *hears* me. When I'm with him, I catch a glimpse of the woman I used to be: the strong, confident, fresh-faced ball-buster I was before this job sucked every piece of joy from my soul.

I've read a lot about this phenomenon. The emotional toll of being a homicide investigator. The statistics are jarring. Substance abuse, suicide, divorce, mental illness, reduced life expectancy—we score off the charts. Something about the demand to stay strong under pressure despite being witness to the most heinous acts a human is capable of. If we crack emotionally, an entire case can unravel, a victim never gets justice, and a killer walks free. The pressure is real.

It gets exhausting.

I should insert here that Kellan and I have not had sex. We haven't even kissed. Although I've considered both many times —mainly the former. It surprises me, this almost animalistic desire I have to make love to this man. It is so unlike how I feel toward my husband. The mere touch of Kellan's skin against mine makes me wet while not even a bottle of lube can prepare me for sex with my husband. With Kellan, it's just different. Everything between us feels natural, everything happens as it should. My body responds naturally to him. If I am in peri-menopause, I've decided that Kellan is my cure.

Or is it that he is my escape from it? Or my escape from something else, perhaps?

We sit in silence for ten minutes, windows down, listening to night slowly move around us. Crickets, cicadas, nocturnals skittering through the trees and under the brush.

Eventually, I turn my head, soak in his profile. The strong, sharp edges.

"Why do you do this?" I ask.

Moonlight is splashed against Kellan's face like warpaint. I like his face in shadow. It brings out the brightness in his blue eyes.

"Do what?"

I gesture between us. "Me. This. Keep meeting me here. Doing this."

His eyes narrow as he considers his response.

"When I was young," he says finally, "my older brother and I shared a bedroom—his name was Jack. We spent a lot of time in there... Our dad, he wasn't really a model father, to say the least. Anyway, his senior year, Jack started sneaking out, and smuggling in booze constantly. He would get really drunk—I mean blackout drunk, nightly. For months this went on." He pauses. "Looking back, I think my brother had depression from a very young age. Anyway, one night, just like all the others, Jack stumbled in the window and fell onto his bed. I woke up the next morning and he was dead. Choked on his own vomit."

"Oh my God."

"I spent a lot of time wondering if he would still be alive if I had told my parents about his substance abuse. If they, or I, had intervened, would he still be alive? If I'd addressed his depression, would he still be alive? I knew he was drinking and acting very differently, and I didn't say anything. I felt like I had a loyalty to him and I didn't want him to get in trouble."

"I understand—more than you know. And I'm so sorry."

"Me too."

I frown, mentally returning to the question I asked that spurred on this terrible story. *Why do you keep meeting me here?*

"Are you saying you see the same depression in me? You relate to me in that way? That's why you keep meeting me? You feel sorry for me?"

"No, Rowan. I'm saying that... that single event changed me to my core. It was a pivotal moment in my life. It showed me—right in front of my face—how fragile life is." He snaps his fingers. "I went to bed, woke up, and my brother was dead. In an instant, we can be gone. So I figure while we're here—while we're *lucky* enough to be here—we owe it to ourselves to make it count. To live in the moment, to follow that tug, that instinct, to explore. It's why I joined the military. I wanted to do something that counts, to serve my country, and I wanted to travel the world. To see things that most of us never will. We have to experience life, Rowan. Not just make it through, but *live* it."

I feel the sting of tears in my eyes. "I'm so much older than you are, Kellan. There are so many other girls in town—"

"I know. I dated all of them when I moved here."

I roll my eyes. He's not joking.

"Rowan, let me ask you something. Why do you do this job?"

"Because it's what I trained for. It's my path. It's where I'm most myself, for better or worse. I don't know," I shrug. "I'm just drawn to it."

"Exactly." He gently runs his knuckle down the side of my cheek.

A rush of emotion floods my chest. I take his hand, kiss his fingertips.

Kellan and I don't speak the rest of the evening.

We don't need to.

EIGHT

AMBER

"Please, sit."

Emma Shaver, my son's first-grade teacher, who also happens to be a dear friend, gestures to the lima-bean-shaped table covered in rainbow construction paper.

I pull out one of the teeny blue chairs that circle the table, but once I notice the curious brown stain in the center, I quickly push it back and grab another.

Mark, my husband, struggles to center himself on his own teeny blue chair. The sour expression on his face confirms what I already know. He is none too pleased that I reserved the seven-thirty spot for our parent-teacher conference. Mark has never been a morning person.

Emma takes her place across from us. The beads around her long thin neck and matching bracelets jangle as she settles into position at the head of the table. Per usual, Emma is boho-chic personified in a tie-dye kaftan that sweeps her tanned ankles. This is in stark contrast to the slate-gray pantsuit I squeezed myself into twenty minutes earlier, and in even greater contrast to the baggy utility pants Mark is wearing, one knee stained with paint. While Emma's long, blonde hair is perfectly braided, my shoulder-length, blonde, curly hair looks like it went through the end of a weed-eater.

I'm in awe of her energy. Emma is one of those women who people are drawn to. She radiates life. It's what attracted me to her when we met at a pre-K fundraiser years ago.

"I'm sorry I'm running a few minutes late," Emma apologizes while gathering papers. She taps them against the desk to straighten the edges. "My seven-fifteen showed up ten minutes late—which is pretty late considering it's only a fifteen-minute meeting." She waves a hand in the air to dismiss the bad energy. "Anyway..."

My husband is scrolling through his cell phone with the kind of focus one might give a nuclear threat. A local handyman emergency that can't wait. I feel the sharp sting of annoyance, disappointment, *embarrassment* that I've felt for how many years now? Seven? Eight?

"Okay, so Connor..." At the sound of my son's name, my attention fixes on Emma—to the purpose of the meeting, to what is *important*. Thankfully, Mark clicks off his phone and slides it into one of the ten pockets that line his utility pants. God, I hate those pants.

"Firstly," she says, her pixie-face sobering, "I'll go through Connor's latest report card." She hands us each a piece of paper. My stomach sinks as I see the ones and twos glaring back at me, where there should be fours and fives.

Emma goes through the song and dance of walking us through each metric. Language, arts, math, science, social studies, specials, and a new section labeled student responsibilities which measures things like if the student uses their time wisely, follows directions, works well with others, follows rules, and strives for quality work.

Mark and I nod in unison as Emma speaks, our eyes glued to the report.

"You can see that Connor's average score is a two. Let me

explain what that means. Ones indicate emergent progress which means attempts are being made—with teacher support—to understand the concepts or skills. A two means that he demonstrates partial understanding of these concepts or skills." She doesn't bother to tell us what three through five mean, because none of those numbers are on his report. But I know from my own research that a number three basically means your child is normal.

Emma glances up, looking between us, indicating that now is a good time for a question. I give my husband the opportunity to step up. To speak. To take a leadership position within our family. To show that he cares.

He doesn't.

I want to slam the heel of my pump into my husband's shin. Instead, I clear my throat and *I* step up—like always.

"Is there anything Connor has improved on since first quarter?" I ask.

"His confidence is improving," she offers, though I know this compliment is a stretch. Connor's confidence has improved only because he is more comfortable with his teacher and surroundings.

Emma continues, "I've seen him take initiative more than he ever has before. And I'm really proud of him for that. However, Connor is significantly behind his peers, and the gap seems to be growing as the year progresses. I suggest having Connor tested to learn more about how he is developing. These are called developmental and behavioral screening tests."

"Where do we do that?" I ask, feeling my pulse increasing.

"Here, in school. It's very easy. I submit the request, pending your approval of course, and then he will be periodically pulled from class for the testing over the next few weeks."

"Approved. What exactly will these tests tell us?"

"The questions are tailored around things like the child's language, movement, thinking, behavior, and emotions. It will give us a broad picture of where he's at, and also if he qualifies for in-school therapy, like speech, occupational, or literacy help."

"Like, special-ed?" My heart is suddenly in my throat.

"No, no, no. Nothing like that. Just... extra one-on-one help. But in addition to that..." She shifts in her seat. Emma has become uncomfortable now, a behavior I rarely see in her. "I spoke with my colleague, Karen Wilson, who you might know—she's been a teacher here for over twenty-five years. She has observed Connor in the classroom over multiple different occasions, and we both agree that we think there is something more than just a developmental delay going on here."

Now my stomach is on the floor.

"For example," she continues, "when I speak to Connor, there seems to be a break in the communication wheel."

"What's a break in the communication wheel?"

"It means there's some sort of breakdown between him receiving what I am saying, and then him processing it..." My heart is now racing. "And then him putting those thoughts into words. There is something not clicking where it should be."

I glance at Mark. He is staring at Emma.

The thing is, we knew something was different with our beautiful baby boy almost immediately. Connor was significantly delayed in every single milestone. Holding up his head, rolling over, eating, walking, you name it. He was (and still is) extremely emotional—abnormally so. He also had terrible colic. Connor was more than just a difficult baby, I somehow knew in my gut. I knew something was wrong but kept telling myself he would eventually grow out of it, that he would catch up to his peers. Months went on, years. At what point do you know that it's time to intervene?

I guess right now.

"Emma," my voice cracks. "What do you think it is? Like, autism?"

"I don't know," she admits. "He displays a few stereotypical autism-like behaviors, but definitely not enough to check that box, in my opinion. He is a loving child who likes to give and receive hugs, and doesn't mind being touched. He thrives while being in a circle of friends. If it is autism, he could be low on the spectrum..." She raises her palms and I notice a new tattoo on her wrist, something artsy. "But I am not a doctor. I am just telling you that I think it's time to explore the fact that there could possibly be something else going on here."

My thoughts are spinning so quickly that I begin to stutter. "So... Where do I... How do I... What do I do?"

"I would suggest going to his pediatrician," Emma says, leaning back in her teeny blue chair. "Tell her everything I said, and whatever else you think could be pertinent, and see what she thinks. Likely, she'll refer you to The Sunshine Clinic, which is a multi-day testing facility that screens for autism specifically. There, you'll be able to rule that out. She will probably also suggest genetic testing, which can uncover any weird mutations in his DNA that could be causing his issues."

"How does it do that?"

"It's a simple blood test. Not a big deal. Then... you just go from there."

"What if he does have autism?"

A warm, heartfelt smile crosses my friend's face. "Then you adapt. He's still your son, he's still a beautiful little boy and you will learn how to adapt to his new needs. But personally, I don't think it's autism, though that is likely where they will start looking."

NINE

AMBER

Mark and I don't speak as we get into our beat-up family sedan. Badly in need of new tires, a new paint job, and at least two belts, considering the screams that come from the engine when it starts up. Mark loves this car. I have no idea why.

I sink into the seat and lean back with a heavy sigh.

As we drive through the school parking lot, I observe the teachers hurrying over the crosswalks. Each has multiple bags hung over their shoulders, and holds brightly-colored travel mugs probably filled with coffee. Each on their way to tell a little boy or girl's parents that their child is totally normal.

There are ten thousand questions I want to ask my husband in this moment.

Why didn't you speak?

If you weren't going to participate, why did you come?

What were you looking at on your phone? What was more important than our son?

What happened to our marriage?

When did we become strangers?

When did you stop loving me?

When did I stop caring?

"What do you think?" I ask as we brake at a red light.

"I think he's in first grade."

Like a flame to gasoline, my defenses ignite. "Meaning?"

"Meaning the kid is seven years old, Amber. School is new to him. He'll catch up."

My jaw literally unhinges as I gape at my husband. Words evade me, because I know that if I press the subject, Mark will offer only a few nibbles of feedback before closing his mouth and returning to the dull, lifeless expression he wears like a mask. And that will be it, the subject will lie dormant until I bring it up again. Me, the nagging wife.

I don't know when, but somewhere along the line, my husband became depressed.

Mark's only interest is his handyman business which he named Blackbird Cove Handyman Services. A name as boring and colorless as our marriage has become. My husband works out of a small, one-room shop downtown that he inherited from his late father; it's where Mark spends most of his life. What he does there, I have absolutely no idea. Certainly not work because last year his total gross revenue was $27,346.90. His net revenue was $-4,394.06.

About a year ago, I decided to surprise him with lunch on a random Wednesday. To my surprise, a customer was in the shop, so I quickly stepped into the shadows and watched from the windows, eager to see my husband in action. Mark smiled and laughed, energetically, jovially, to the elderly man inquiring about new cabinets for his kitchen. That was the day that I realized that my husband hadn't checked out of life. He'd checked out of his family.

We ride in silence the rest of the way home. The drive takes twice as long with the morning school traffic, the extra time only adding to the tension swarming like bees around us. Actually, I'm not sure Mark even feels the tension anymore, only I do.

Mark rolls to a stop at the curb and jumps out to get the mail, causing a soccer mom to blare the horn and flip us the bird as she zooms past in her minivan. Her bumper sticker reads: *Powered by Jesus.*

As we accelerate up the driveaway, my gaze drifts to a beam of sunlight shining on the statue of the cartoonish frog that sits next to our red front door. A meditation frog, the tag read. I purchased him at a festival downtown three years ago, hoping the symbol of peace would transfer into the home. So far, no luck.

I stare at the statue that I love so much—his little frog hands folded across his lap, his legs bent in a meditative position, his eyes closed, the small curve on his mouth—and I wonder when I allowed my life to become so bleak.

The garage door jerks before grinding open. We slowly roll inside. The smell of motor oil fills my nose. It grinds back down.

Leave it, leave it, leave it, I internally tell myself, regarding the bills. *Leave them for him.*

When he doesn't grab the mail, I am so mad that I don't even want to walk into the house with him. So I push out of the car, and ignoring my husband, kick off my shoes, and make my way to the mess that has taken over the second bay of the garage.

Mark disappears inside the house, shuts the door behind him. The moment he is gone, I exhale, feeling the weight release from my shoulders.

"Okay," I say to no one, fisting my hands on my hips. I have a few hours until my first appointment of the day. I stare at the stacks of boxes and old office furniture and supplies that were once in my office.

I remember the day I opened Bailey Counseling. Me, owner and CEO. Me, entrepreneur, mom, wife, soon-to-be on the cover of *Forbes* magazine. The headline: *She Can Do It All*. It was *mine. I* had done this. Me, me, me. Finally, all the years in college, dragging myself deeper into debt, were going to pay off. I was overflowing with pride, hope and accomplishment.

And then I couldn't pay the bills. The rent and liability insurance alone were astronomical. Between the cost of running a business, and being unable to pay for any office help whatsoever, I was slowly drowning. I made the tough decision to close Bailey Counseling after only two years in business. Now, I work for a local group practice called Oak Tree Counseling.

Do I feel like a failure? Yep. But do I sleep better at night knowing the entire business isn't on my shoulders? Yes.

It's been almost a year since I closed my doors and I still haven't done a thing with what remains of my old office.

Until now.

I open the garage door, inhaling the sweep of cool, fresh autumn air that blows in with it. Several leaves dance inside, settling at my bare feet. I consider running inside to change clothes, but don't even want to see my husband. So, I unbutton the top button of my slacks, roll up the pant legs, and shed the jacket.

After selecting a playlist from my cell phone and putting it on blast, I lower into a crisscross on the garage floor and begin.

Two hours and two boxes later, I decide to take a break from scanning and redirect my focus on something less mind-numbing. I grab the fabric cleaner and go to work on the couch we are planning to sell. It's a beige two-seater with an eggshell-colored wavy print that I bought on Craigslist. Nothing special, but it was conformable and nice enough to serve as the client couch in my office, where countless patients spilled their deepest and darkest secrets to me.

The playlist switches to Lizzo and I begin humming, my shoulders dancing with the beat.

That's right, Lizzo, it's time to focus on me.

I reach between the cushions and pause, my fingers finding the corner of something hard.

Frowning, I pull out what appears to be a small, thin notebook.

Inside there is no name, no date, just pages and pages of barely legible scribblings.

TEN

ROWAN

The early morning sun streams through dusty windows, the slanted shades casting long lines across the boardroom table. The conference room is boiling hot, an unfortunate side-effect of being located next to the station's main furnace. Despite it being only eight-thirty in the morning, the Blackbird Cove Police Department is a buzz of activity. It always is after a homicide. Especially one as gory and sensational as Alyssa Kaing's.

Crammed around the pockmarked table is my partner, Kellan Palmer, our admin officer, Evelyn Weber, and Sergeant Chris Hoffman, a mid-thirties, competent officer who I hand selected to help on this particular case.

It is officially day one of our investigation.

I set down my coffee—black with three packets of sugar— and seat myself at the head of the table. All eyes turn to me. My stomach roils with nerves. Maybe coffee wasn't a good idea.

I plug in my laptop to the projector, power it up, and slip into my role as lead detective. Into the only role in which I am competent. On that note, I begin.

"Thanks for meeting on such short notice." I take a quick

inhale to steady my voice. "Let's dive right in. Chris, will you hit the lights, please?

I click into the crime scene photos. The horrifying image of Alyssa Kaing's mutilated face fills the projector screen.

"First, we will discuss the nature of the homicide. I should start by saying—clarifying, rather—that we are working under the full assumption that this *is* a homicide. That this was not an accident, nor suicide. Therefore, we are living, eating, and breathing three things now: means, motive, and opportunity. These three buckets will frame every single conversation we have about this case, got it?"

Nods around the room.

"Okay, here we go. According to Darcy, the victim was strangled—you can see the purple contusions around her neck— and we are assuming that this is how the assailant disabled her, and that this is also the cause of death. From the initial examination there appears to be no sign of a struggle, either in the room or on Mrs. Kaing's body. This makes me think she either knew her assailant or that the assailant snuck up on her and took her by surprise."

I zoom in on Alyssa's face.

Evelyn, the only other woman in the room, gasps.

"Sorry," she apologizes quickly for the outburst, folding her hands neatly over her notebook. Today, her long acrylic nails are adorned with little white flowers, an update from the kitten paws she had last week.

"As you can see an X has been carved over each of Mrs. Kaing's eyes. Darcy thinks this was done postmortem with a small paring knife, or maybe even a scalpel. Whoever did this took their time and clearly wanted the X to be prominent. Other than the eyes, there are no obvious signs of other mutilation." I click to a picture of her arms. "Important to note, it appears that there are needle marks around her median cubital vein, and also, that they don't appear to be recent. She also has an anarchy tattoo which she tried to coverup with roses. Both these things suggest a rebellious past. Darcy is going to run a toxicology scan to see if there were any drugs in Alyssa's body at the time she died. Next, the scene." I nod to Kellan to take the reins, as we'd planned. Kellan is alert and impeccably dressed in a starched blue dress shirt and slacks.

You would never know he was up with me until almost four in the morning.

ELEVEN

AMBER

I wait until Mark goes to "work" to open the mysterious notebook I found in between the couch cushions.

I take a sip of coffee and settle in behind the kitchen table. Only nine-thirty in the morning and I'm already exhausted.

My first client meeting of the day starts in thirty minutes. Typically, I would be in the office by now, reviewing patient files, but my curiosity has gotten the better of me.

I trail my finger along the worn, blue cardboard cover. It reminds me of those cheap, flimsy notebooks provided in school. Again, I search for a name, but come up short.

I open the notebook and, inside, I find pages and pages— *and pages*—of scribbled writings. Most are almost illegible.

I raise from the table and grab my reading glasses from the cabinet. Even then, I have to squint to make out each sentence.

The notebook appears to be a food diary, or log, of sorts.

Frowning, I turn back to the first page. It is broken into blocks. One labeled *Bfast*, one labeled *Lunch*, one labeled *Dinner*, and one labeled *Feelings*.

Page one reads:

Bfast: Coffee – black, no sugar, no creamer. Xanax.
Lunch: 4oz cup of yogurt, organic, no sugar. Coffee, black, no
sugar. Apple cider vinegar.
Dinner: Protein shake. Wine. Coffee. Xanax.

I wrinkle my nose. An extremely unhealthy diet, and also, rather alarming. I cringe to think of what kind of state the woman's stomach lining is in—and her nervous system for that matter.

Next, under the header of "*Feelings,*" are multiple lines of disjointed half-thoughts. They read:

I woke up still fat.
4+ pounds heavier today. How is that even possible? Current
weight, 105.
Eyes swollen, puffy.
Throat hurts.
Lightheaded, vibration feeling in body.
Pissed, foul mood.
Workout – stacked twenty-minute ride onto a thirty-minute.
Twenty push-ups, thirty sit-ups.
Canceled manicure today. Too embarrassed. My nails are
disgusting. They're brittle and frayed and one is bloody from a
hangnail I ripped last night.

Another entry:

Feelings: I hate my life. I want to run away and never come back.
I want to start over, somewhere no one knows me.
Today, 104 lbs.
Workout – forty-five-minute HIIT, afternoon upper body
weights.
Feel like shit, again.

*Today I almost passed out at the gym. I had to lie down in the
bathroom for twenty minutes. It was so gross.*
I'm gross.
I hate my life.

Another one:

*My hair is falling out. It's so thin the sun shines through the
strands in pictures. I'm going to shave my head. Like Britney. I
feel like that sometimes. Like I'm screaming for help but no one
hears me.*
I'm going to get on hormones.
Call doctor tomorrow.

I flip though the next handful of pages, which are more of
the same. The writings of a mentally unwell anorexic woman—
the stereotype of most of my forty-plus patients.

My phone beeps, alerting me to a text message. I glance at
the clock. I'm going to be late to my meeting.

I close the notebook and hide it in a crock pot in the cabinet.
I needn't worry, Mark never cooks. After grabbing my purse and
packed lunch, I dart out the door.

For the entire drive to work I think about the notebook, and
wonder who it belonged to.

Why do I get such an uneasy feeling when I read it?

TWELVE

ROWAN

Kellan begins his update. "There was no sign of forced entry anywhere in the home. So, either the doors were unlocked and the assailant walked right in, or, as Rowan mentioned, Mrs. Kaing knew her assailant and willingly let him or her into the home. There were also no viable footprints or boot prints anywhere inside or outside the home. The Kaings do have a security system, but according to my buddy at the security company, the system was not active on Monday, nor any of the surrounding days. He said they rarely turn it on."

I click to a picture of Alyssa and her husband Zach that I screen-shotted from social media. "Zach is the chief operating officer of a new startup tech company called Zeus Technologies Inc. He's currently in Japan for business. Interesting note, Hoyt informed me that Mr. And Mrs. Kaing have been trying to have a baby but have been unable to conceive." I clear my throat and look away, my pulse beginning to increase.

"Have you verified that the husband is, in fact, in Japan?" Evelyn asks.

"Yes, I've left a voicemail with his assistant. I've not heard back; I'll let you all know when I do. At this point, we have no idea if Zach knows his wife is dead."

Sergeant Chris Hoffman raises his calloused hand. "Tell me more about this witness and his connection to the victim."

I click to a picture of Amos Hoyt that I found on the internet, taken during a local Veterans Day parade. "Amos Hoyt is a seventy-one-year-old former marine." I flick a glance to Kellan. "He's a widower, his wife died of breast cancer three years ago. Two weeks ago, Alyssa gave Hoyt a key to their home to use in case of emergencies, and he also has her personal cell phone number."

"The victim gave her neighbor a key in case of emergencies two weeks before she was murdered?" Sergeant Hoffman frowns.

"Exactly." I shift my weight. I'm beginning sweat. "It makes me think that Alyssa might have known something was coming. If so, what? With who? These are all things we need to find out."

"How often did Hoyt see her?"

"I'm not certain. He said they kept running into each other at the edge of their back yards and struck up a friendship."

"Feels odd."

"I know. I agree. I bluntly asked him if they had a romantic relationship. He emphatically said no."

Suspicious gazes flicker across the room.

"How reliable is this Hoyt guy? Health-wise? Vision, brain, that kind of stuff?" Evelyn asks.

"Good question." I quickly wipe the beads of sweat from my forehead, feigning an itch. "I spoke with him myself inside his home. He seemed alert, lucid, quick-witted. Healthy, strong. I think he's a neighborhood watch kind of guy, and also, that he likely knows more than he's telling us."

Kellan interrupts. "Like, he's the real killer and used his key to walk right in."

I nod. "We can't ignore that option, I agree. But, remember, he also had her trust. Enough for her to give him a key to the home and her personal cell number. She trusted him."

"So did Ted Bundy's victims."

I cock a brow. *Good point.* "I also noticed a joint in an ashtray. Normally, I wouldn't think much of it, but considering the needle marks on Alyssa's arm, I can't ignore the drug connection there. Might be nothing, might be something, I don't know. That said, I definitely want to dig into him more. I'd like to find out who his medical doctor is, see if he has a prescription for medical marijuana, and also if he has any cognitive issues, which would negate his statement. Evelyn, can you please own that task?"

Evelyn nods, scribbles in her daisy-printed notebook. Always the same notebook, always the same pen.

I switch focus to my notes. "I've got the chief requesting a warrant for the victim's cell phone records. I'm hoping for that tomorrow."

Sergeant Hoffman flicks his hand into the air. "You said that we don't know if the husband knows his wife is dead. But she's been dead for over two days—why isn't he alarmed that he hasn't heard from his wife in over two days? Why wouldn't he have called us for a welfare visit?"

"I thought that very thing. Something is strange there for sure. We need to dig up everything we can on Zach Kaing. Any criminal records, social media, where he went to school, his résumé, his extended family, I want to know everything I can about him. I want to know if there was a life insurance policy on his wife, and if so, how much."

"Do you have any reason to believe that he is involved here?"

"Not at this moment, no."

I click back to the image of Alyssa's body. "Let's shift gears now. I want us all to take a moment to discuss the mutilation."

The room falls silent. Evelyn shifts uncomfortably in her seat.

"Her eyes were X'd out. This is either the killer's M.O.—modus operandi—or meant to be some sort of message for us."

"According to the search I ran," Kellan adds, "there are no crimes in the area, past or present, where the killer carved eyes. So I don't think we're looking for a serial killer with that particular M.O. I think this guy lives in this area and this is his first kill. Call it a gut instinct."

"Agreed. Let's consider the message angle." I click to the next slide. "I did a bit of research on the symbolism of X and highlighted the ones that jumped out to me. An X symbolizes the end of something, like death. Do you remember those old cartoons where the dead characters had X's over their eyes? Like that. There are also spiritual and occult meanings. X can also mean 'marks the spot,' like in a treasure hunt. Lastly—I found this one interesting—X is the symbol of a kiss."

"Or could it be that she saw something that she wasn't supposed to." Evelyn offers.

I take a note. "Yes... absolutely, good job. Perhaps Mrs. Kaing saw something that she wasn't supposed to and was killed for it."

When no one else has anything to add, I continue. "So what does this tell us?"

The faces in the room are blank.

"It tells us that this is an emotional murder. Something as particular and risky as a postmortem carving suggests the killer had an emotional motive. It is likely someone Alyssa knew, and someone who felt wronged by Alyssa. This is punishment for something she's done."

"Or something she saw," Evelyn presses her theory.

I nod. "Could be, yes."

"So this helps narrow down the pool of suspects," she says.

Kellan raises his hand again. "Again, I'm looking at Hoyt."

"Hang on," Hoffman interrupts. "You mentioned she was trying to have kids and couldn't. This could be a motive for the husband. Maybe it's punishment for not being able to bear his children?"

"Pretty fucking harsh punishment," Kellan scoffs.

"Agreed," I say, "But, yes, that's something that can't be overlooked. But again, if he was out of the country, it makes it less likely that he is the killer—and also, it doesn't allow for either means or opportunity."

"He could have paid someone to do it."

"Fair point."

"What about her family?"

"Tracking them down is one of the first things I'm going to do today," I glance down at my notebook, overflowing with a hundred little scribbles. Thoughts, theories, facts, a random Christmas tree. "I'm going to identify who they are and inter-view them personally. Her maiden name is Smith and she was born in Houston, so I'll start there. My plan is to have a solid victim profile by lunch, going all the way back to junior high school."

"Somebody has to know something."

"I agree, somebody always knows something." I glance at the clock, and give a quick recap, assigning duties.

"What about the media?" Kellan asks. "They're going to be swarming us by ten o'clock."

"Send them to me."

"You got it."

I close my notebook. "Remember we need motive, means, and opportunity. We have no case without hitting all three. I need solid facts, solid information."

Nods around the room.

"Let's meet again at four-thirty today. Each of us should have an overload of information by then. Right now, I'm going to the morgue to check in on the autopsy."

Kellan stands. "I'll ride with you."

THIRTEEN

Interview Transcript 5

Participants:
Special Agent Darla Thatcher, PhD, ABPP
Case 927-4 "RS"

Thatcher: Did you catch the game last night?

RS: Yeah.

Thatcher: Good, huh?

[No response.]

Thatcher: Did you see that home run at the end?

RS: Yeah.

Thatcher: What do they call that again?

RS: A grand slam.

Thatcher: That's right. Thanks for schooling me. You know baseball better than anyone I know, you know that?

[No response.]

Thatcher: Did you watch it in the shelter's community room?

RS: Yeah.

Thatcher: Great. I'm really proud of you. The more you hang out in there, the more comfortable you'll be around the others. I'm really, really proud of you.

[No response.]

Thatcher: Did you visit your new school last week?

RS: Yeah.

Thatcher: Did Miss Leslie take you?

RS: Yeah.

Thatcher: Awesome. Tell me about it.

RS: It's a lot bigger than my old school.

Thatcher: I bet. First-graders need a lot more space. I think you've grown an inch in height just in the last few weeks.

[No response.]

Thatcher: What was your favorite part of the new school?

RS: The gym.

Thatcher: Gym class was always my favorite, too. Are you going to sign up to play baseball next season?

[No response.]

Thatcher: Can you look at me, please? … Thank you. Are you going to sign up to play baseball?

RS: Yeah, I think so.

Thatcher: I think that would be great. Hey. I was thinking, today let's draw. What do you think?

RS: Draw what?

Thatcher: Well, considering we seem to be on a baseball theme, how about a baseball field and everything that goes along with it? I've got tons of stuff in this big ol' bag I carry. Let's see… White paper, construction paper, crayons, markers—I think I even have some glitter in here… No glitter, huh? Okay, cool kid. Let's draw.

Thatcher: Who's that your drawing?

RS: Babe Ruth.

Thatcher: Wow! Fantastic. Looks just like him. Okay, so you've got the diamond and players, how about we draw the audience in the stands now?

Thatcher: Who is that?

RS: Me.

Thatcher: You've got one heck of a seat, kid. I hope you brought your glove... Ah, yes, I see it there now. Who is that next to you?

[No response.]

Thatcher: Can you tell me who you drew next to you?

[No response.]

Thatcher: Okay, fine. Can I ask this guy some questions?

RS: Who?

Thatcher: You, in the picture. Sitting right here behind home base.

RS: Okay...

Thatcher: I understand this young man has had a bit of a rough time lately, is that correct?

[No response.]

Thatcher: I heard that he hasn't been treated very nicely. Is that true?

[No response.]

Thatcher: Can you help him out and speak for him? Tell me what happened to him? This young man here?

[No response.]

Thatcher: There are a lot of people that love this guy a whole bunch, and we can't wait to see all the wonderful things he is going to accomplish in his life... like maybe becoming a pro baseball player.

RS: They're called major league players.

Thatcher: Ah. Thanks. What would I do without you? You know, I think Babe Ruth had a tough childhood, just like this young man sitting behind home base, and in order to make room for all the wonderful things that would happen to him in his life, he had to talk about the bad things and then move on from them. So, maybe this young man here can talk about the bad things. Can you tell me what happened to him?

RS: Bad things.

Thatcher: Ah. So just like Babe Ruth, then. I understand. Can you describe those bad things to me?

[No response.]

Thatcher: Okay, let's try this. I'm going to point to different parts of the boy's body and ask him some questions, okay?

RS: Okay.

Thatcher: Did anyone ever touch the boy here?

RS: No.

Thatcher: Did anyone ever touch the boy here?

RS: No.

Thatcher: Good, because that's where the funny bone is, and that would feel, well, funny. How about here?

RS: No.

Thatcher: Here?

RS: Yes.

Thatcher: How did that make him feel when he was touched there?

[No response.]

Thatcher: Did he feel uncomfortable? Maybe like a bunch of butter-flies in his stomach? Maybe a little nervous and sick to his stomach?

RS: Yes.

Thatcher: I'm sorry. How about back here—back there? Did anyone every touch him back there?

RS: Yes.

Thatcher: And how did that feel?

RS: It hurt.

Thatcher: I'm so sorry.

[No response.]

Thatcher: How many times was he touched, in a way that hurt him or made him feel uncomfortable?

RS: A lot.

Thatcher: Does he remember when it started happening?

RS: A while ago.

Thatcher: A few weeks, or like, a long time ago?

RS: A long time ago.

Thatcher: Do you remember how long specifically?

RS: No.

Thatcher: Okay. I'm going to pull out some pictures and I'd like you to point to all the people who touched that little boy in an uncomfortable way, okay?

RS: … That one.

Thatcher: That one?

RS: Yes.

Thatcher: Are you sure?

RS: Yes.

FOURTEEN

ROWAN

"What a beautiful day."

I cock my brow at Kellan. "Only you would say that while we're in the middle of a homicide investigation."

"You have to compartmentalize, Rowan. Look around, take it in. Step out of death for a moment."

After an overly dramatic roll of my eyes, I look up at the sky. It's sapphire blue speckled with big, fluffy white clouds. To our right, the lake laps lazily against the shore, and to the left, the woods are ablaze with autumn. A light, seventy-three-degree breeze sweeps over my skin like silk. It is a pretty afternoon. A welcomed change from the hellish morning we've had.

Kellan and I spent hours tracking down Alyssa's friends and family and, so far, have gotten zero useful information. Alyssa is estranged from basically everyone in her past. Once a wild child, it appears that Alyssa matured and turned over a new leaf, cleaned herself up, and found herself a millionaire, leaving her past far behind.

An hour ago, Kellan suggested we take a break from the mundane calls and drop in at the Kaing house to see if Hoffman had found anything useful. He was assigned to go back to the crime scene and conduct a second walk-through.

It was Kellan's idea to park at the top of the neighborhood and walk up the shoreline, skirting the back of the houses, a route that the killer possibly took.

"You need a vacation," Kellan says abruptly.

I snort. "Are you serious?"

"Yes. When was the last time you took one?"

"Never."

"Never?"

"Yeah."

"That's crazy."

"Says the twenty-something single bachelor."

"I'm a few months from thirty, and everyone needs a break. If you could go anywhere in the world right now, if everything around you could just pause for a moment, where would you go?"

"Paris."

"No kidding?"

"Why are you so surprised?"

"I don't know, most people would say somewhere with a beach."

"Not me. I've always wanted to go. See the Eiffel Tower, visit the Moulin Rouge, eat my weight in crepes."

"I'd like to see that last one."

"I bet you would. How about you? Where would you go?"

"I'd take you on that trip to Paris."

A smile catches me and for a moment—a single moment—I feel like a little girl. Giddy and love-struck. It reminds me of the way I felt when I first met Shepherd.

"Come on," Kellan pivots from the path and gestures me onto a dilapidated pier known as Piper's Pier. The rotted planks extend fifty feet into the lake and ends with a T, where fishermen often spend entire days. Today, it is vacant.

Together, wc walk to the end and peer into the murky, black water.

"How many dead bodies do you think are in there?" he asks.

"A lot. More than you'd think."

"Why do you say that?"

"There's a strong undercurrent that runs through this area of the lake, swallowing up and carrying debris all the way to the center, which drops almost three hundred feet deep, and is about a mile wide."

"So you're saying it's a perfect place to get rid of evidence."

"Exactly."

"Should we send divers out?"

"And tell them to look for a four-inch surgical scalpel that severed Alyssa's eyeballs? No. Not yet. Let's get more solid information first." I take a dccp breath and a shudder catches me. "God, what a creepy murder."

"Tell me about it."

I stare at my reflection in the water, distorted and dark. A chill rolls up the back of my spine. Suddenly, I want nothing more than to get away from the water. I grab Kellan's arm. "Come on, let's go, we've got work to do."

Once back on the shoreline, Kellan pauses to squint at the houses in the distance, barely visible through the trees.

"Is that the neighbor's house? Amos Hoyt?"

I frown, look from left to right to get my bearings, then study the piece of the large brick home I can see through a narrow break in the trees. I can just make out the deck that extends from the master bedroom—the one speckled with binoculars and marijuana joints.

"Yeah, I think it is his house."

"Let's go talk to him."

"No, let's check on Hoffman first. He's expecting us."

"No, I want to meet this mystery Hoyt guy. He'll see us at the Kaings'. I want to drop in when he's not expecting us."

I fist my hands on my hips. "You think he did it, don't you?"

"He checks the boxes for both means and opportunity. He's the one constant in this case."

I gaze up at the house, remembering the feeling I had that Hoyt was withholding something from me.

"Alright, fine. Come on."

Amos Hoyt answers the door on the second ring, wearing a long-sleeved flannel shirt, slacks, boots, and a newsboy cap. He's either just returned from running errands or has been expecting us all along. Something inside me assumes the latter.

"Detective Velky." His calloused, gnarled hand slips into mine. Then, he turns his focus to Kellan, eyes narrowed with curiosity.

Kellan stretches out his hand. "Detective Kellan Palmer. I hear you're a marine."

Hoyt's bushy brow cocks with interest. They shake hands. "Yes, sir."

"Same."

And just like that, I no longer exist.

Hoyt invites us inside, and while he and Kellan fall into easy, casual conversation about their time in the military, I stay a few steps behind, scanning each room as we pass—looking for what, I'm not sure.

Hoyt leads us to the kitchen. "Would either of you like some coffee? I just put on a pot."

Simultaneously, I say *no,* while Kellan says *yes.*

Always accept hospitality from a witness, it makes them more comfortable, I once told Kellan, my own words slapping me in the face.

After pouring Kellan a cup of tar-black coffee, Hoyt leans against the counter and we get down to business. Kellan takes the lead, which is just fine with me.

I listen as Hoyt recites the same story he told me when I interviewed him the night before. Exactly, almost word for word. Except...

"I do remember something else, in addition to what I told Detective Velky last night..." Hoyt flickers a glance to me, shifting his weight.

"What's that?" Kellan asks.

"I do remember Alyssa saying something along the lines that she thought someone was following her."

"*What?*" I snap, stepping away from the window and closer to the conversation.

Hoyt nods. "Sorry, I just remembered." He shifts again. He's nervous. I glance at Kellan who shoots me a look—*Cool it. I've got this.*

"Who was following her?" Kellan asks.

"Don't know. I don't think she knew."

"Tell us exactly what she said."

"Exactly that. Nothing else really. She said that she thought she saw someone in the woods, staring at her house, and the same person again in the parking lot of the grocery store, then at the post office, and a few more times in the woods."

I blink, shocked and angered that he didn't tell me this during our initial meeting.

"Did she describe the person? Man or woman? Height? Age?"

"She wasn't sure, that's all she said."

I am literally biting the inside of my cheek with frustration.

"Did she know what this person drives?" Kellan asks.

"No—I asked that specifically. She said she always just saw them in the distance."

"She was sure it was the same person, each time?"

"Apparently."

"When did she tell you this?"

"Uh," Hoyt tips up his newsboy cap and scratches his white

hair. "A few months ago. Never brought it up again. I also noticed someone walking around the neighborhood recently. It stuck out to me because they were alone and wearing white— not jogging clothes or whatever. That's all I could tell, and no, before you ask, I don't know if it was a man or a woman. Could've been anything really."

I frown at Kellan, then focus back on Hoyt. "Mr. Hoyt—"

"Amos."

Jesus. "Amos, why didn't you tell me all this last night?"

"I didn't remember."

"I don't believe you."

Kellan glares at me.

Hoyt stares at me for a minute, like he's assessing me, then seems to decide something. "She told me not to tell anyone, ever."

"Not to tell anyone that she thought someone was following her?"

"Right."

"Why?"

He shrugs. "I don't know. But I'm a loyal man, in life or death. Kellan understands this."

Hoyt holds Kellan's gaze for a moment and I feel like I'm out of the loop.

Kellan dips his chin. "Thank you for the information, Amos. Is there anything else?"

"No."

"Okay, if you do think of anything else," he pulls a card from his pocket, "please call me immediately."

"You have my card, too," I blurt like a petulant child.

Amos nods. "I'll walk you two out."

"Why the hell wouldn't Alyssa want anyone to know that she thought she was being followed?" I hiss as we step onto the sidewalk and out of earshot. "That makes no sense. Right?"

When Kellan doesn't answer, I slap his bicep. "*Hello?* Kellan?"

"I'm thinking, hang on."

I make it three more steps before hitting him again. "Talk. I feel like I'm about to explode. What are you thinking?"

"One of the assumptions we have is that Alyssa's eyes were X'd out because she saw or did something she wasn't supposed to, right? So, if she reported that she was being followed—or if Hoyt did for her—then that means that cops would come to her house and ask questions. And *that* means there would be attention on the Kaing household."

"Meaning, whatever secrets she has, or whatever she's hiding, might come to light."

"Right. And that secret might have gotten her killed."

We walk a few minutes in silence, mentally rolling over this new information.

"I can't believe he didn't tell me this when I interviewed him," I grumble.

"It's because you're not a man," Kellan winks.

"You're joking."

"Nope. I know his type. Macho, sexist."

"Unbelievable. God that's so antiquated."

"It is what it is. You have to find a way around it."

"How?"

"Keep me with you. At all times."

As he says that, an icy intensity darkens his eyes. It's then that I realize Kellan isn't glued to my hip today so that we can make the best investigative team possible, it's because he's concerned for my safety.

FIFTEEN

ROWAN

Thirty years earlier

"What's your name?"

Those were the first words Shepherd Velky ever said to me.

I remember looking up from the textbook I was studying and my stomach falling through the bottom of my feet. Not just to them, but through them. It was like one of those movie-moments where the boy enters the room in slow motion, the wind blowing through his hair, the sun sparkling against two rows of perfect white teeth.

It was a frigid January day. A thin layer of ice framed every window of the foster home—as if the environment wasn't cold enough. I was in the "reading room" which consisted of two folding tables, plastic chairs, bookshelves, and posters that read things like: If You Can Dream It, You Can Do It. Shepherd was wearing a beat-up leather jacket with one pocket peeling away as if he'd torn it on the Harley he'd rode in on. That's how I imagined him, anyway. A Harley-driving heartthrob.

I'll never, ever forget that moment. It changed the course of my life.

"Rowan," I squeaked out, then quickly cleared my throat. "My name is Rowan."

The boy smirked, a cocky smirk, like he knew what he was doing to my hormones.

"Rowan; that's a weird name."

I didn't respond. It was weird.

"I'm Shep," he said and thrust out his hand like a grownup.

"Shep? That's a weird name." I slid my hand into his, feeling a rush of nerves as he squeezed and shook. His hand was warm, despite the cold.

"It's actually Shepherd, but everyone calls me Shep."

I smiled—not too big—and tucked a strand of hair behind my ear. I'd read somewhere that guys liked when women played with their hair.

Shepherd tilted his head to the side, regarding the textbook between my hands. "What are you studying?"

"Social studies. I have a test tomorrow."

"What grade are you in?"

"Sixth."

"I'm in seventh. You want some help?"

The butterflies in my stomach suddenly spun into a tornado of nerves.

"Sure."

The boy named Shepherd grabbed a plastic chair from a nearby table, flipped it around, and straddled it next to me. You know, the way the bad boys always sit in the movies. A waft of musky body spray followed a second later and every sensor in my body ignited.

"Ah." He pointed to the textbook. "Give me your pen."

I did, and he highlighted the section entitled The War of 1812. "When they ask you to write a paper on a major turning point in America, choose this. I wrote a paper on it. I can give it to you."

His eyes twinkled as he smiled at me.

"Okay." I looked away for fear he'd see the blush on my cheeks. "Thanks."

We pretended to read for a few minutes.

"How long have you been here?" he asked finally.

"Eight months."

Eight months, eleven days, and four hours, to be exact.

"Is this your first time here?"

"Yes."

"You're lucky."

I frowned. "What do you mean?"

"This is one of the nicest children's shelters in the area."

One of the nicest? He had to be kidding.

"How many have you been in?" I asked.

"Five. This is my second time being transferred to this one."

"Transferred?"

"The one I was in filled up. The longer you stay, the more they move you around."

I blinked. I couldn't imagine being shuttled between children's shelters. Wasn't being in one bad enough?

"How long have you been in the system?" I asked, feeling an immediate connection to him now.

"Six years."

We stared at each other for a minute. There was no pity, no sympathy. No 'I'm sorry, that's awful.' Because, to us, this was life. We didn't know any different. We only knew what was. Abusive parents, horrific living conditions, neglect, famine, shame. Survival to us was becoming, quite literally, nothing. Silent, still, and out of sight. That was what childhood was to us.

People don't understand that. It's like being born with a disease, it sucks—you know this because society tells you it does —but you don't know any different. You adapt because you have to. And while some of us are forced to stay in these abusive households, others are removed and entered into "the system." The government becomes our parents. Our identity becomes tied to a case file and number. There, we are no longer told to be silent and hidden, in fact, we are pressured to talk to therapists, to engage with the other kids, to do chores, to participate. Here we will be shuffled from one facility to the next, from one foster home to the next, constantly moving, constantly meeting new faces, constantly being told that we're safe despite not knowing a single person around us. There is no stability when you are in the system. None. Every day you wake up wondering when the rug will be pulled out from under you next, all the while dealing with however the trauma of the past has chosen to manifest in your body.

When I met Shepherd, he had been in the system for years. I'd only been in eight months. I was a newbie compared to him. A noob, he called me.

After helping prepare me for my social studies test, Shepherd closed the book, looked at me, and, inches from my face, said, "Stick with me kid. I'll take care of you."

Never, in my life, have I clung onto anything more than those five little words.

SIXTEEN

AMBER

Dos Tacos is a small, locally owned Tex-Mex restaurant located in downtown Blackbird Cove, a block away from Mark's handyman shop. It's one of my favorite spots—the restaurant, not his shop, to be clear. Particularly, the outdoor patio that was built around a hundred-year-old oak tree. Every single branch is wrapped in strings of lights. It's beautiful at night. On "Taco Tuesdays," they have a mariachi band. A real mariachi band with trumpets, violins, and guitars. The musicians wear traditional three-piece suits and wink when you tip them. I love it.

I have chosen our usual spot, the back corner table, inches from the tree trunk. It's the only table available. The patio is packed, locals and tourists flocking to the outdoors to celebrate the stunning autumn weather.

The door swings open and Emma hurries across the patio, kaftan flowing, hair braided. The men turn as she passes. She hangs her beaded purse on the back of the seat as the waiter walks up. He's new, I note, mid-twenties with long brown hair tied into a man bun, and bored bloodshot eyes that suggest he's only just awoken, despite the fact that it is three-thirty in the afternoon.

"I'll take a Miller Light," Emma says.

The waiter nods, looks at me. "Margarita on the rocks."

What's the mark of a good friend, you ask? One who doesn't judge when you order a tequila in the middle of your workday. I still have two more client appointments to get through.

Emma sinks into the chair. It feels like forever since our early-morning parent-teacher conference, and she looks unusually tired.

"Tough day?" I ask, my mouth watering as the waiter slides a bucket of beer onto the table next to us.

"I had two kids throw up," she scowls, squeezing a blob of antibacterial gel on her hands. "Literally thirty minutes apart. All over our reading carpet. One on one end, one on the other. The room still stinks."

"Gross."

"I know. They have the stomach flu."

I dramatically propel myself against the back of my chair and cross myself.

Emma laughs and shakes her head. "No, don't worry, you're good. I had it last week. No germs here."

"Thank God. You know that the norovirus can live on door knobs for five days?"

"Girl, please—I know."

"Speaking of last week... You had another date, didn't you? We haven't talked about that yet. Fill me in. I need gossip." I also need her *not* to bring up Connor and how she thinks something is wrong with my son. I'm still processing, and quite frankly, don't want to talk about it.

The waiter delivers our drinks. We both pause to take long, deep sips.

"How did it go?" I press, licking the salt from my lips and feeling the tingle of goosebumps over my skin.

Emma pauses.

A grin spreads across my face. "Oh my God, that good?"

"I don't know—I don't really want to talk about it."

"Oh my—you like him? You actually like this mystery guy?"

"He's..." Her cheeks flush. "I don't know yet, Amber."

"What's his name?"

Emma vehemently shakes her head. "Nope, not until I'm sure."

I laugh, roll my eyes. Emma has this thing of not "naming" a man until she is certain he's going to stick around for a bit. As a therapist, I know this is a defense mechanism triggered by the need for self-preservation; I get it.

Emma has never been married. She is two months shy of her thirty-second birthday and, if I had to guess, is beginning to feel her clock ticking. I know she wants kids; she just hasn't found the right man to procreate with. Honestly, I feel bad for her. My best friend is a free spirit, has lived a wild and crazy and unrestricted gypsy life, and now it seems that life is passing her by.

"Promise you'll keep me updated on the guy?" I ask when I realize she's not going to indulge me.

"Promise. Now. How's Mark?"

I immediately drop my eyes. I have a visceral reaction to hearing my husband's name.

"Mark is the same," I deadpan. "Nothing ever changes with him."

"What did he say about my assessment of Connor this morning?"

"*Ulch*," I sink back in the seat. "Nothing. He said freaking nothing, Emma."

"I'm so sorry. What an ass. He didn't have *any* insight or thoughts about it?"

"No." I take a deep breath. "Oh, and by the way, I called the clinic you referred us to take Connor to. It's a four-month wait to even make an appointment for an autism assessment."

Emma's jaw drops. "Unbelievable."

"I know. But I did speak with his pediatrician and, considering the autism stuff is going to take so long, I asked if she would put in a rush order for genetic testing. They just called and we were able to snag a cancellation spot for tomorrow morning."

"That's fantastic. Information is power." Emma pauses. "Connor had a good day today. He was calm, focused, and he participated in class. Oh, and I sent in the request for the testing at the school. Hoping to get that scheduled for some time next week."

"Good."

"Where is he now?"

"He's with Gladys."

Gladys is Mark's mother, Connor's grandmother, a four-foot-nine seventy-two-year-old widow with zero filter. Literally, the woman will vocalize whatever comes into her head at any given moment. She lives two doors down from us, and has a terrible habit of stopping by unannounced. But the bright side is that she's willing to babysit Connor when Mark can't, until either Mark or I get home from work. I have no idea what the two do together, but it's free childcare.

"Anyway," I say around a salty sip. "I really don't want to talk about Connor—or Mark—anymore."

"Good because I don't want to talk about kids and emotionally unavailable men either."

We laugh and I feel the tension begin to slip from my shoulders.

Emma's phone beeps and as she checks the message, my attention is pulled to the table next to us. A table of twenty-somethings, sharing a bucket of beer and a vape pen.

"...dead body was found."

"Where?"

"Mirror Lakes—you know that really rich neighborhood on the east side of town?"

"Yeah. Dead, as in, died of natural causes or was, like, murdered?"

"Murdered. The cop my buddy talked to said it was pretty bad. She was like, strangled and tortured..."

Emma is eavesdropping now too, both of us wide-eyed, staring at each other.

"Did you know about this?" I whisper.

"No." She glances over at the table, debating on asking the strangers for more details—Emma is the social butterfly of this duo—but she decides against it. Instead, she sips and shakes her head. "So creepy. This town has changed so much. It's not small and safe anymore."

"Yeah." I make a mental note to check the news on my phone later, then say, "You know what else is creepy?"

"What?"

"I found a notebook in the cushions of the couch I used to have in my office at my old counseling clinic."

"Oh, that's right—you're doing the garage sale soon, right?"

"Yep. Next weekend."

"What kind of notebook? Like a journal or diary?"

"Yeah. But not really a diary, more of a food journal. Like a diet tracker."

"A diet tracker?"

"I know; kinda weird."

"Whose is it?"

"I have no clue. There's no name in the notebook but I'm assuming it belonged to one of my old clients. A very disturbed old client."

"Do you recognize the handwriting or anything at all about it?"

"Nope. I think it's a woman's writing, but that's it. But the writings in it... I don't know, there's just something about it that gives me the creeps. I can't put my finger on it."

"Did you tell Mark?"

"No." I shrug.

Emma stares at me, sympathy pulling her face. "Amber, talk to me. Just get it out."

I feel an instantaneous sting of tears, the kind that bubble up and are impossible to control. The kind that seem to come out of nowhere, a space buried deep in your psyche where emotions go to die. Except they don't die, they release like a flood when you finally enter a safe space.

Emma leans forward and grabs my hand. "Oh, Amber, I am so sorry. Honey, cry if you need to, who gives a shit? I'm sure you're not the first person to cry in a Mexican restaurant."

I sniff, swipe the tears with the back of my hand. "Dammit," I mutter, "I'm so embarrassed."

"Don't be. You've got a lot going on right now. You've got a scary situation with your son. Something unknown, not understood. And your marriage is... well, awful. It's okay to cry. And, like I've suggested, it's also *okay* to visit with a divorce attorney, just to understand the process, should it come to that. Listen, I know someone. I'll send her a message and just put some feelers out there. See if she can work you in."

I suck in a breath, shake off the tears. "Yeah, I think... I think it's time."

"Good. Just take a little step, and see how it feels."

SEVENTEEN

ROWAN

"It's four-thirty, time for the call," Kellan reminds me, closing the passenger-side window.

"Yep," I say, distracted. "You ready?"

"Yes—no, wait." Gently, Kellan takes my chin, turns my face away from my email and says, "Take a deep breath. We've got this." I close my eyes, melt into the butterflies that only he can give me, and then take a deep breath.

He smiles, pulls away. "Now we're ready," he winks.

After taking an inhale to steady my thrumming heart, I secure the phone into the dashboard holder and dial into the conference call I'd emailed to the team an hour before. The meeting is meant to serve as an opportunity to touch base on the Alyssa Kaing homicide.

The cab is silent as Kellan and I wait for Evelyn and Hoffman to join the video call. I don't worry about them seeing us together; they know Kellan has been assigned to shadow me practically everywhere.

An image of the conference room pops up on the phone, followed by Evelyn's ruddy, smiling face and Hoffman's trademark frown.

"Hi, guys," I say. "Is it just you two in the room?"

"Affirmative," Hoffman says. Evelyn nods, flipping open her daisy notebook.

"Great. Okay, let's start with Chris. Give everyone an update."

"I spent over four hours walking the Kaings' home, double-checking the locks, the windows, looking for tire tracks, anything that might indicate a break-in. There is nothing. From my assessment, whoever killed Alyssa either had a key—like the neighbor does—or the doors of the home were unlocked and the assailant walked right in, which, in this neighborhood isn't hard to imagine."

"Agreed," I say.

"I also think they parked at another location and walked up—there's just too many prying eyes in this neighborhood and I don't think our suspect is that stupid. They possibly came up through the woods, or along the sidewalk, or the shoreline of the lake. There is a neighborhood park about a quarter mile from the Kaing home which would be a perfect spot to park a vehicle and blend in. I'm working on gaining access to the CCTV cams there; I'll let you know when I get them."

"Good call. What about fingerprints in the home?"

"Well, as suspected, the tech said the home is covered in fingerprints considering people live there. He dusted a few from the window locks and door frames, sent them off, but I don't feel good about it. I wouldn't recommend putting too much stock in obtaining anything useful from this angle. That's my update."

"Got it. Evelyn, what do you have for us?"

"I found out who does the Kaings' housekeeping. It's a regionally based company called Angel Cleaners, LLC. They were a tough nut to crack, let me tell you. Because of confidentiality reasons, they wouldn't give me information right away. I had to threaten a warrant and spook them by telling them that the information I need is related to a homicide. So, FYI, you might get a call about that."

I grin. Despite all her pink and daisies, Evelyn is a dog with a bone. Nothing will stop her from obtaining what she's got her eye on.

She continues, "I have a call into my personal friend who is a nurse at Cove Clinic. I'm going to see if she can peek into the neighbor, Amos Hoyt's, medical file to see if he's got any cognitive or mental health issues—oh, also, he has no criminal record, FYI. I confirmed that. Anyway, I'm waiting on my nurse-friend to call back with the medical information. I'll let you know."

"Anything on the autopsy?" Hoffman asks us.

"Darcy is conducting it as we speak," Kellan says. "We did get the toxicology report, and at the time of Alyssa Kaing's death, she was clean of drugs."

"Interesting. So, the altercation is not likely drug-related."

"Right."

"I'm getting the picture that she is rehabilitated and cleaned up," I say, then switch gears. "Okay, here's our report. Kellan and I spent most of the day speaking with Alyssa's friends and family, and canvassing the Kaing neighborhood. Nothing useful from her friends and family, but we did get a hell of a nugget from Amos Hoyt, after dropping by his house. He told us that Alyssa told him that she felt like someone had been following her in the months leading up to her death."

Hoffman sits up, Evelyn cocks a brow.

"Don't get too excited, that's literally all we know. Alyssa wasn't sure whether it was a man or a woman, because she only saw the person from a distance, and told Hoyt that she saw this person several times outside her home and also in town—she thinks."

"Hair color, race, height, anything?" Hoffman presses.

"Nope." I flip open my notebook. "The big news is that we finally spoke with Zach Kaing, the husband. He says he is still in Japan on business. Before I told him that his wife had been murdered, I asked if he had spoken with her recently. He said that he hadn't, in a few days. I think this is strange. When I told him his wife was deceased, and that it appears to be from suspicious causes, he seemed to be genuinely surprised. Speechless, actually. But I didn't get the sense of a lot of love lost. He's booking the first flight home."

"And coming here for an interview?"

"Yes."

"What questions did he ask?" Hoffman leans forward, steepling his hands in front of his face.

"Typical stuff: Do we know who did it, how did it happen, etc. I kept the details as short as possible, and told him we're waiting for the autopsy for more information. I did *not* tell him about the Xs over her eyes. I'm saving that for face-to-face so that I can see his reaction. We exchanged information and he texted right before I walked in here saying he was already at the airport and should be landing back in the states tomorrow afternoon. He's going to come straight to the station."

"Do you believe him?" Evelyn asks. "What does your gut say?"

"TBD. I requested that he send me his flight information, which he did, so I do believe that he is out of the country, which makes it impossible for him to have physically killed her. As for my gut..." I hesitate. "I'm not sure... Something definitely seems off."

"Him being out of the country doesn't mean he couldn't have paid somebody to do it," Evelyn adds, stuck on the husband angle.

"Right." I flip a page in my notebook. "So, the next big thing is the autopsy—getting those results. And then we'll talk to Zach Kaing immediately when he returns to the states tomorrow afternoon. Does anyone else have anything to add?"

When no one speaks, I wrap up. "Okay then, let's sync up

again tomorrow morning at the office, let's say eight o'clock. But if anything comes through before then, call me. The CCTV footage, the housekeeper..."

"You got it."

"Are you guys coming into the office now?" Hoffman asks, his eyes shifting around the cab of my vehicle.

"No, I've got a few things to do. I might come in later tonight, we'll see." I look at Kellan.

"I'm not sure yet," he says to the group.

I disconnect the video call.

Kellan looks at me. "My bet's on the husband or the neighbor."

"It's always a man, isn't it?"

"Always. Men are such pigs."

I grin, but it feels forced. I'm tired, my head feels swimmy from not eating enough food, not drinking enough water, no sleep.

Kellan slides his hand on my knee. "Want to grab some fast food real quick? I'm starving."

I glance at the clock. "I can't. I have an appointment."

"An appointment?"

"Yes."

"What kind of appointment?"

"A personal one." I start the engine.

Kellan's brow cocks. "A personal appointment with who?"

"With none of your business."

Kellan's gaze lingers, but he doesn't press, doesn't argue, and also, doesn't remove his hand from my leg.

EIGHTEEN

AMBER

I am sitting behind my desk, enjoying my margarita buzz while scrolling through my favorite clothing app, when the desk phone buzzes.

"Mrs. Bailey, your five o'clock is here," Susan, the Oak Tree Counseling's office manager croons though the speaker. Susan is twenty-two years old, and has the voice of a porn star and the attention span of a Goldendoodle. It's a confusing combination.

I glance at the clock. *Shit.* Time got away from me. Or maybe I should say, the tequila got me.

"Thank you, Susan," I say into the phone speaker. "Give me five minutes and send her back."

I quickly minimize the clothing app (currently with a $327 cart) and take a moment to center myself. My desk is a mess. My breath smells like booze, my mascara is smudged. I've got two missed texts from Mark, the last informing me that he's going to be working late again. I roll my eyes and don't respond. Instead, I run my finger under my eyes, then switch focus to the file labeled DET. ROWAN VELKY.

I'm midway through scanning the first paragraph of my notes from our last session when I hear footsteps down the hall.

I make a mental note to buy Susan an egg timer because that definitely wasn't five minutes.

With the best warm smile I can muster, I open the office door.

"Hey, Rowan."

Rowan nods and breezes into the small room I call my office. Always in a hurry, always busy, always fidgety. Rowan is one of those type-A's who lacks the ability to relax. It's one of the things that makes her good at her job. She's always "on."

"Have a seat," I offer as I round my desk.

Rowan sits on the left side of the couch, next to the door, the farthest distance from me that the space will allow. This is where she sits every time, even when she used to come to my old office. Rowan is my only client ever to sit in that exact spot. Everyone else chooses the seat directly in front of me. It's a painfully obvious—albeit subconscious to her—physical display of her need for a smooth exit. To run from anything that becomes too uncomfortable. In this clinic, the exit serves as Rowan's security blanket.

"So," I begin, "how are you?"

"Busy."

I nod, taking in the detective in front of me—or awkwardly, at a forty-degree angle, I should say. Rowan is a beautiful woman, though she has absolutely no clue of this. A natural, unassuming beauty. The golden highlights in her long, brown hair compliment a caramel skin tone that women spend hours in tanning beds to achieve. She has a sexy, sultry look to her. My guess is she has either Native American or Latina in her lineage. Her style, however, is, cringe-worthy. Always an ill-fitting dress shirt and slacks, always thick soled shoes that remind me of the men and women in the Silver Sneaks program at the local senior center. But today, something is off. Her demeanor is different, her eyes a bit wild. Skin a bit pale. She seems exceptionally fatigued and tired.

"Tell me about what's got you so busy?"

"I've got a new case." She regards me closely, waiting to see if I've heard the news. I recall the gossip I overheard earlier this afternoon with Emma—the bits and pieces I can remember, anyway.

"Ah, yes. I heard something happened at Mirror Lakes? Someone died. Is that what you're talking about?"

Rowan nods and fidgets with the hem of her shirt. "It was a homicide."

"Wow. So that's got you working nonstop, then."

She nods.

I allow the silence to linger between us, hoping that it won't be one of *those* visits again. My first meeting with Rowan Velky was mandated by law, after she was involved in an officer-involved shooting. Rowan shot and killed a fifty-year-old Caucasian male, high on methamphetamine, who was wielding a machete behind the local gas station. She was cleared of any wrongdoing, but had to fulfill her end of therapy. Once our mandated five sessions were up, I assumed I would never see her again. I was wrong. For reasons unbeknownst to me, Rowan requested to continue our therapy sessions. And here we are. She, staring out the window, me, trying to crack one of the thickest nuts I have ever come across.

When I realize it is, indeed, going to be one of *those* sessions, I take a deep breath and refer to my notes.

NINETEEN

AMBER

"How is your Aunt Jenny doing?" I ask, looking at the note I'd scribbled and circled ten times: *sick aunt – jenny.*

Rowan fills me in on the latest details of her aunt's dementia. This is a triggering topic for her.

Rowan spent most of her childhood and early teenage years in children's shelters and bouncing in and out of foster homes. Both of her parents were drug addicts, meth to be exact. I only know this information because it was in her file when she was referred to me after the gas-station incident—not because Rowan voluntarily offered the information to me. I'm glad I was privy to these details beforehand because it helped me understand why Rowan felt no remorse for ending the machete-wielding man's life. None whatsoever. I suspect this emotional vacuity is a direct result of the trauma she suffered while growing up in a drug-addicted environment. An emotional wall, so to speak.

During her tumultuous childhood, Rowan's aunt was the only family member who offered to foster Rowan, but when her aunt fell into financial hardship and had to file for bankruptcy, only six months after moving her niece in, she surrendered

Rowan back to the system. I suspect Rowan has taken Jenny in now because she feels a sense of loyalty to the woman, not because the two are close.

I note that Rowan doesn't mention her husband once in the Aunt Jenny update. So, I steer the conversation, as the intricacies of her marriage is something I am exhaustively trying to peel back.

"How are things with you and Shepherd?"

Rowan considers her answer.

"The same," she says finally.

"How so?"

"He still doesn't have a job, and for whatever reason, won't accept any that has been offered to him. And I still don't ever want to have sex with him. And we still fight constantly. And now, he's drinking way too much."

"What was your last argument about?"

"Sex, money, and me being a workaholic."

"Okay, so same argument, new day."

"Exactly."

"And how did this one end?"

"I went to work."

I snort.

Rowan smirks. A rare thing. She's pretty when she smiles.

"Rowan, during our last visit we talked about high sensation seekers, a very specific personality type."

"I remember."

"I want to dive into this a bit more. As we discussed, sensation seekers constantly crave new experiences, whether good or bad. Not just stereotypical things like jumping off cliffs, or racing cars, but smaller things like trying new restaurants, signing up for the latest and greatest whatever, or maybe constantly buying new things. We talked about how you moved from apartment to apartment every six months after you turned eighteen—for no apparent reason other than you simply wanted to. And how you jumped from job to job until finally settling at the department. You've stayed in this job because it offers something new and exciting—for lack of a better word—almost daily. It's the perfect job for you. Every time you get a new case you get that dopamine rush, and you commit yourself fully to it until it's closed. And then you get another, and another…"

I pause for feedback. I get none. I'm not sure if she's accepting my analysis of her personality or is simply ignoring me.

"I asked you last week what marriage felt like to you and you said a cage. You said it felt like being in a box with all the sides taped down. That's a pretty big statement."

Still, nothing.

"Sensation seekers often feel this way when things begin to become mundane or too routine—as marriage tends to become. Last week, I asked you a very simple question: Do you want to leave your husband? You didn't answer then; I'm hoping you'll answer now."

There's a long moment of silence.

"No," she says.

"Why?"

"I don't know."

"Yes, you do, somewhere deep down you know the answer to that question and it's my job to pull it out of you. Let me ask you this: Do you not want to leave your husband because you feel guilty about breaking the vow of a marriage? Or maybe hurting him in the process? Or is it that you truly love him?"

No response.

"Or maybe it's none of that—maybe it's that you don't want to leave what marriage provides for you. Is Shepherd an anchor of sorts? Whether you fight or not, do you find solace in the fact that he will always come home to you no matter what? Does this give you a sense of security?"

Her brows raise ever so slightly. "Yes... I think—I do feel that way."

"So that's what I want to dig into. There is something inside you that desperately needs security and stability, despite the fact that you are a sensation-seeking personality. And whatever this is, is a dominant thing in your life. I'd really like to understand the whys of this."

"I think he might be cheating on me," she blurts, momentarily stunning me but also sending a rush of relief through my body. Finally, something to dig into. However, I'm also surprised by this confession because I have had a hunch that *she* has been cheating on *him*. I've just been waiting for her to tell me about it. It fits with her sensation-seeking personality type, and is alarmingly common in that subset of people. Oftentimes the man or woman may be deeply in love with their spouse, but the insatiable need for fresh experiences drives them to cheat. It's a very difficult situation to untangle, for all players involved.

I say, "Thank you for telling me this. This must be extra hard on you, because if he is cheating, this is a threat to the sense of security you crave so badly. What makes you think he's cheating on you?"

"Call it a gut instinct." She shifts in her seat. "He constantly goes out with his friends, but comes home later and later each time. And he avoids me after. He's also more distant than ever. Also, he's stopped bringing up wanting to have kids."

Her cheeks flush, though her expression remains hard. I'm proud of her. I know it was difficult for her to open up like this, and the fact that she did tells me that this topic is weighing heavily on her mind.

When Rowan first started talking about her marriage, babies were the first topic. Her husband wants them badly, she does not, although the *why* is still to be determined.

"Have you confronted him about this potential affair?"

"No."

"What would be the first thing you would say if you did?"

"How dare you. That's what I would say." Her jaw clenches, unable to control the anger. "Loyalty is everything to me, and he knows that. In a world where so many bad things happen, having someone stand by you, especially in your worst moments, can be the difference between a good life and a bad one."

"So this loops into what we were just talking about. Maybe you don't want to leave Shepherd because of the high value you place on loyalty. The security Shepherd provides you—that you need—is rooted in loyalty. You feel a sense of loyalty to both him and to what he provides you."

"Yes, I'd say that's accurate." A sour expression pulls her face. She tilts her head to the side. "Do you know what else I'm mad about?"

"What?"

"That he thinks I wouldn't find out. I'm a freaking *detective*. It's literally my job to identify and uncover clues, to solve mysteries."

"So it feels like a slap in the face to what you love the most—your job."

"I guess you could say that. Feels like he doesn't even respect me enough to consider that I might find out."

"Or is it maybe that he doesn't care? Maybe he's at that point in your marriage—he doesn't care if you find out."

Rowan looks at me, the implication tough for her to digest.

"The only way we can answer these questions is if you ask him about it, Rowan."

The detective nods, but then goes quiet.

A minute passes.

Another.

I glance at the clock. Ten minutes. We are only *ten* minutes into our session. We have forty minutes left to fill.

This is how it goes. Rowan comes in, sits far away from me,

doesn't speak, until I eventually prompt her with open-ended questions, which usually lead to her husband. I'll get twenty minutes out of her tops, and that's it. We sit in silence the remainder of the appointment.

For months this has been going on.

There is something Rowan needs to get off her chest, something that keeps her coming back.

TWENTY

ROWAN

My head throbs as I pull into the driveway. Therapy does that to me.

Night hovers above the treetops, slowly pushing away what remains of daylight. The days are growing shorter. I shift in my seat, closer to the open window, and inhale deeply. The evening has grown cold, the air stinging my lungs as I suck in a breath, hoping to clear the headache.

The light glowing from the kitchen window tells me that Shepherd is home. I roll into the garage, cut the engine, take another deep breath. My headache has now wrapped to the back of my head.

When I open the door, I am taken aback by the fresh scent of rosemary and thyme.

I hang up my purse, slip out of my jacket, then make my way to the kitchen. Banjo surges up from the floor and rushes me, licking my hand. His tail is wagging so hard his entire back end sways from side to side. I reach into the dog-cookie jar and give him a treat. Satisfied, he trots back to his pillow and resumes his rest.

The evening news murmurs from the small television

tucked under the corner cabinets. Shepherd is standing at the counter, mincing garlic and onions for a soup that is simmering on the stove. A fresh loaf of French bread sits next to a half-drunk glass of wine.

Over his shoulder he says, "Hey."

"Hey. You're cooking."

"Yeah."

"Where's Jenny?"

"In her room, watching *Judge Judy*."

"How was she when April dropped her off?"

"Fine."

I step past him, grab a wine glass, and pour what remains of the wine (not much) into my glass.

A beat passes between us.

"It's my first glass," he lies, his tone laced with annoyance.

"I wasn't going to say a word."

"Yeah right," he mutters as I pass.

I turn around, a rush of anger blowing through my system. "Are you serious right now? I just walked in the freaking door."

Shepherd's jaw twitches. He begins mincing faster.

I close my eyes and silently inhale. Then, "I called a place today, a facility, that cares for people with Alzheimer's. It's in Dallas."

"For Jenny, you mean?" *Ta, tap tap tap tap*, the knife viciously pelts the cutting board.

"Yes. I know it's been hard on you having her here."

No response.

"Anyway, I'm waiting on them to call me back and we'll go from there."

"Who's going to pay for this facility for your aunt?"

My jaw drops. "Listen, Shep, I'm doing this *for you*."

He scoffs.

"This is me trying to make things better between us. Do you not see that?"

"Who's going to pay for it?"

"I don't know!" I throw my hand into the air. The wine sloshes from the glass in the other, splashing the toe of my boot. My ugly she-let-herself-go shoes. "Insurance, maybe, I don't know. Jesus Shepherd, you—"

"Fuck!" The knife tumbles from his hand, clattering onto the tiled floor. Blood gathers on the white cutting board, speckling the garlic.

I slide my wine on the counter and follow as Shepherd hurries to the sink, having to side-step Banjo who is interested in the sudden burst of commotion.

"Are you okay?"

"No I'm not okay! I cut my freaking finger." Ugly hives form around his neck.

He's shaking—with anger or adrenaline from the pain, I'm not sure.

"Here let me—" I try to take his hand but he jerks it away.

"Just get the fuck away from me, Rowan. *Shit.*" He rears back, shoving his heel into Banjo's ribs.

I stumble back, grab Banjo's collar. "*Hey,* you just kicked Banjo."

"He was trying to jump on me."

Speechless, I watch my husband wash the deep gash next to his fingernail.

It's then that I see it—a small tattoo on his wrist. A *new* tattoo, peeking out from under the band of the watch he never takes off. As the soap rinses away, the shape reveals itself. The tattoo is of a V balancing on an upside-down triangle with an X in the center. A symbol of sorts.

"What is that?" I ask.

"What?"

"On your wrist."

He glances at his hand. "Nothing."

"Did you get a new tattoo?"

No response.

My pulse picks up, that gut instinct surging to life. "What is it, Shepherd? What is that tattoo?"

"God, Rowan, just leave me alone. *Please*."

"Fine." I grab my wine, spin on my heel, and call for Banjo.

I find myself pausing in the hallway. I don't know where to go. I don't want to see Aunt Jenny, I don't want to go to the bedroom Shepherd and I share, and I don't want to sit in the living room which is adjacent to the kitchen. My home, my sanctuary, is turning into a place where I no longer want to be.

My throat suddenly feels like it's constricting. Tears well in my eyes. I feel like I'm on the fringe of a panic attack, which only makes it worse. Frantically, I swing open the door closest to me—the basement door. After fumbling with the light switch, I stumble down the steps, Banjo at my heels, barely making it to the couch before the tears bubble over.

An hour later, I hear the door slam, Shepherd's truck fire up, and the garage door open and close.

Three hours later, he returns.

I wait until my husband is passed out in bed before opening a new text.

> Me: You up?

> Kellan: Yes.

> Me: Alone?

> Kellan: Of course.

> Me: I'll see you at The Cliff in 15.

TWENTY-ONE

AMBER

It's two in the morning. I can't sleep.

After ensuring Mark is deep in slumber, I slip out of the blankets, and quietly pad out of the room.

I tiptoe to Connor's bedroom and slowly open the door. Moonlight pools on the hardwood floor, illuminating a new baseball glove, probably from Mark's mom. I cross the room to the twin-size bed in the corner.

Connor is still asleep, curled into a ball under the red flannel comforter that's at least two sizes too big for his bed. His soft, chestnut-brown hair is sticking out from all angles and it makes me smile. Inhaling, I cross my arms over my chest and lean down. His sweet angel face is peaceful.

"Keep sleeping well, my baby," I whisper, then make my exit.

I tiptoe downstairs and retrieve my laptop briefcase. After turning on the stove light, I fill a glass of water and slide into a seat at the kitchen table.

I pull out the mystery notebook I found in my old client couch and begin thumbing through the pages.

Entry after entry, filled with daily logs of what this mystery person ate, drank, and how many Xanax she took. Incoherent writings of a woman who, I believe, has a severe case of anorexia, coupled with anxiety and depression. By now, I have built an image of the woman in my head—and it's not pretty. Eating disorders are extremely common, and most common in wealthy or affluent populations. The illness is typically triggered by cultural pressures, skewed perception of one's weight or body type, or traumatic events. I have treated women with this illness in the past. One was a woman who had recently lost her mother, with whom she was extremely close. The woman was jarringly skinny but unaware that she had developed an eating disorder in her attempt to regain a sense of control over her life. She could control food, and therefore became obsessed with it.

The personality types of those who are more likely to experience eating disorders are typically anxious, obsessive, perfectionist, and achievement-oriented.

So, with all that in mind, I'd say the owner of this mystery journal is an affluent woman in her mid-forties with generalized anxiety disorder and several unresolved traumas in her life. Perhaps she is in the throes of a mid-life crisis, though is unaware.

I spend a few minutes trying to recall previous clients that fit this description; but I can't quite place her.

I flip the page, skim through the logs.

Bfast: Coffee. Black, no sugar, no creamer. Xanax.

Lunch: 1/2 apple with 1 tablespoon of peanut butter. Coffee, black, no sugar. Apple cider vinegar and ashwagandha root.

Dinner: Protein shake. Vodka. Xanax.

Feelings: I feel crazy. Sometimes, I really think I'm crazy. When

I don't feel like I want to cry, I feel like I want to drive my car into a telephone pole. I feel like a slug, weak, and lightheaded, but also like a tornado is spinning in my body. Like my bones are rattling underneath. I think I need to make an appointment with doc to increase the dosage of my Xanax. Or maybe switch to valium?

Workout: HIIT and hill ride, upper body strength training, ten-minute sit-up circuit.

On and on the logs go until about midway, my fingers stop on a page that appears to be less of a log and more of a diary entry of sorts.

It reads:

A weird thing happened today. I don't know if I'm going crazy or if maybe I already am crazy.

I was in the gym—the new gym we just built down the hill from the house. I'd just gotten off the rowing machine. It's a rainy day, so it was dark and gloomy outside, making it seem much later than four o'clock in the afternoon. I felt a weird feeling, like that creepy feeling that someone is watching you, and I suddenly felt scared. Very scared. I was only in my sports bra and leggings so grabbed a T-shirt and pulled it on. I peered out the window, and although the view was distorted by the rain running down the glass, I didn't see anyone or anything. But I was too scared to leave the gym and walk back up to the house alone. So I turned on some music and tried to focus on finishing my workout.

Five minutes later, something hit the window, a loud pop that scared the shit out of me. Like maybe a rock or something. I screamed and ran into the bathroom. A few minutes later, I made myself come out and check the window again. Still no one.

At that point I was so freaked out that I wanted to run back to the house rather than stay in the gym. After clicking off the lights, I grabbed my water bottle, but as I turned, I saw something in the mirror. A reflection. Behind me, someone stood outside the window, just a few feet from the building, with a black coat and hood pulled over their face. I froze, completely terrified. I couldn't move. They stared at the back of me, motionless.

Finally, I spun around to face the window, my heart in my throat. But the person was gone.

I re-read the entry two more times, a memory tickling my brain, but I can't pin it. My stomach has gone uneasy, as if an instinct is screaming at me. Frowning, I stare at the page and try to talk myself out of the feeling of doom that has settled in my stomach. The woman likely *is* crazy, and based on the amount of benzodiazepine she takes on a daily basis, also possibly delusional. And besides, what can I do about it now?

I set the notebook aside. I need to check my emails, get back to bed, and try to get some sleep.

After logging into my laptop, I click on the email icon. Slowly, the new mail downloads, populating the screen one by one. A few are from clients, a few spam, two bills, and lastly, one from Emma, sent just thirty minutes earlier—at 2:32 a.m. I click on it.

Hey girl. I just heard back from my divorce lawyer friend. She can work you in next week. The retainer to meet with her is 500 bucks, but she said she'd give you the friends and family discount of 250. (Her daughter is in my class 😊).

Below is her email address. She's waiting to hear from you. I'm proud of you, Amber. Life is too short. This is the hardest part. Just make this one step. And then the next, and then the next.

Let me know when you email her. And let's meet up for drinks this weekend.

I copy the email address at the bottom of the message and open a new email.

My fingers freeze on the keyboard.

My gaze lifts to the framed picture on the wall, one of me, Mark, and Connor, at the beach. Instead of feeling a stab of pain and fear, I feel a rush of courage. I *am* doing the right thing.

Just make this one step.

Heart pounding, I type an email to the divorce attorney and hit send before I can think about it.

I click back into Emma's email, click reply.

I did it.

I lean back, smile.

I. Did. It.

Now, to prepare.

I click into the browser. The tabs are many, each with a different Google search: *what is autism, how to care for a child with autism, does my child have autism, something is wrong with my child, child developmental delays, what causes developmental delays, how to get a divorce.*

My computer dings with a new email alert. It's from Emma, a GIF of two women jumping around with an exploding bottle of champagne. Below it, in all caps:

GOOD JOB, I'M PROUD OF YOU.

I grin, pick up my phone and click into my text messages.

> Me: You're up past your bedtime, young lady.

Emma: wine emoji

> Me: laugh emoji, with who?

Emma: A boy

> Me: Gross. You'll get fired for that

Emma: laugh emoji Ew. Not funny

Emma: He's a man

> Me: Phew. date?

Emma: kind of

> Me: It's time you tell me about this boy-man. We need to meet soon. I want to hear all about it.

Emma: Yes. I need to talk.

> Me: Everything okay?

Emma: yeah, I just need my free therapy sheesh with my bf

> Me: this weekend?

Emma: yes. I'll text after school tomorrow.

> Me: Sounds good

Emma: Did you schedule the autism test?

> Me: yes - six freaking months out

Emma: damn, I'm sorry

Me: it's okay. Tell the boy-man to go home. You need to go to bed. You're going to be hungover.

Emma: kiss emoji

My smile turns into a frown as I stare at the phone. It's unlike Emma to be up past nine, and this makes me even more curious about this mystery man.

I click out of the text conversation and return my focus on the how-to-divorce article.

One step at a time.

TWENTY-TWO

ROWAN

Twenty-eight years earlier

The moment my eyes opened, I flung off the covers and surged out of bed. Wearing a ridiculous grin on my face, I grabbed the robe from the back of the bathroom door and slid into a tattered pair of fuzzy flip flops.

Despite the adrenaline rush, I paused at the bedroom door, and reminded myself to be quiet. Those were the rules. No noise in the house before 8 a.m. Pamela and Ed Jenkins, my current foster parents whom I'd been with for three months, were very strict. I didn't mind this so much because I was just thrilled that they didn't have kids. I was the only child in the home, and this was a scenario I greatly preferred.

I hurried down the rickety wooden staircase of the old farm-house, the steps groaning under my weight. Swinging myself around the bottom banister, I ran to the kitchen.

I stopped abruptly at the doorway, waiting for fanfare.

Pamela and Ed looked up from their bibles, clearly startled at the usual burst of energy from me.

Ed frowned in disapproval.

My gaze frantically searched the kitchen.

"Come sit," Ed demanded curtly in a thick southern drawl. "It's time for the morning's bible lesson, and since you fell asleep before last night's, you'll do two studies this morning."

I blinked, refocusing on my foster father. My stomach dropped to my feet and a wave of sadness washed over me like death.

They'd forgotten my birthday.

My thirteenth birthday. The one where I officially became a teenager.

Swallowing the knot in my throat and choking back the tears, I nodded, "Yes, sir."

My cheeks burned as I lowered into the kitchen chair.

"Sit up," he said, sliding the bible they'd gifted me across the table. "We're on Philippians..."

The phone rang.

Pam pushed out of her chair and answered it. Her eyes snapped to me and I strained to listen to the other end of the conversation. They had a cordless phone, turned up to max volume.

"...we've finally got a room opened up, so we're ready to take her back, as you requested. Are you sure you don't want her? I suspect the overcrowding here is going to continue and we might need to move more children around in the foreseeable future. We greatly appreciate your willingness to help out—"

"Yes. We're sure."

"Okay then, I'll get everything ready for the transport..."

I looked down and began sobbing.

TWENTY-THREE

ROWAN

"How long have you and Alyssa been married?"

"Four years."

Zach Kaing folds his hands on the table, his expression focused but dispassionate, his spine pin-straight, his navy suit impeccable. From the moment Alyssa Kaing's husband walked into the police station, he's exuded confidence, affluence, and power. If not privy to the information beforehand, I would not have believed this man had been traveling for almost twenty hours straight, and is certainly jet-lagged. I am also more curious than ever of how this tech tycoon and the tattooed, needle-scarred Alyssa came to be husband and wife.

Sitting next to Zach is his attorney, a New Yorker named Dennis Patrick. The men share similar dispositions. Dennis is wearing a tailored three-piece suit that probably costs more than my SUV. He has thick white hair and a sharp look in his eye that would intimidate a less-seasoned detective.

Zach, Dennis, Kellan, and I are in the conference room where I have updated Zach on the gory details of his wife's homicide as well as details of the investigation—the ones I chose to share with him, anyway. We now are past the initial bullshit mandatory questions and beginning to dip our toes into the trickier questions. Thus far, Dennis has been silent, which I appreciate.

"Can you tell me what you were doing in Japan?" I ask.

"Yes. I and several of my colleagues were there to meet with potential investors."

"Investors in your company?"

"Yes, Zeus Technologies."

"How long have you been with Zeus Tech?"

"Three years, but I've been in the tech field since graduating college. I can give you my résumé, if you need to document all that."

"No, it's fine, thank you. When did you leave for this latest trip?"

"Last Thursday."

"Was that the last time you saw Alyssa?"

"Yes. Well, the day before, technically. The night before. We had dinner together, said our goodbyes, and she went to bed. I left the house at four the next morning to catch a 6 a.m. flight out."

"So you didn't sleep in the same bed that night?"

"Irrelevant." Dennis speaks. "And his schedule has already been verified, Detective."

"Yes, it has. Just covering the bases. Okay, so you last saw your wife Wednesday night. When did you last speak to her?"

For a second—*a split-second*—Zach looks down. He quickly corrects this misstep and returns his focus to me.

"Wednesday night at dinner was the last time I spoke with my wife."

"You didn't wake her to say goodbye before you left Thursday morning?"

"No."

"And you didn't speak to her after that?"

"No."

"Not once?"

"No."

"So, just so that I understand, you left for an international trip and didn't bother to check in with your wife a single time while you were gone—not even when you landed to tell her you were safe?"

"That's correct."

"May I ask why?"

"It's really not abnormal for us, especially when I travel. She knows I'm busy."

"How about text messages?" Kellan asks from the corner of the room where he's standing, arms crossed over his chest. "Not even a single text?"

Zach shakes his head. "No."

An awkward silence lingers in the room. Yes, it is extremely abnormal that a man would travel internationally and not be in communication with his wife—but it does not make him a murderer.

"Do you know if your wife had plans while you were out of the country?"

"I'm not sure. She mentioned gardening and I'm sure she went to her Pilates class. But, no, I don't know of any specific plans."

"Who are Alyssa's closest friends?"

"She has a high school friend named Julie, who I think she keeps in touch with. But other than her, none that I'm aware of. She's kind of a loner."

"What about enemies?"

"Enemies?"

I nod.

"No, Alyssa didn't have any enemies."

"Think for a moment: Is there anyone that she might've mentioned who made her mad, or perhaps she made them mad? Friends, family? Think. Even something as mundane as an incident at the grocery store. Or pulling out in front of somebody—road rage, whatever. Is there *anything* she mentioned recently?"

Zach thinks for a moment then shakes his head. "No."

"Alyssa does not have an ex-husband, correct? She didn't marry before you?"

"That's correct."

"What about ex-boyfriends?"

"Of course she had ex-boyfriends."

"Would you mind giving me their names?"

"Those I know of, sure." Zach offers two names, which I scribble on my notebook.

"Mr. Kaing, I know this might be uncomfortable for you, but I need to ask a few things that pertain to the manner in which your wife was killed."

His eyes remain ice cold.

"We spoke about her eyes and how they were mutilated. Does the letter X mean anything to you? Or to her?"

"No."

"We have multiple theories we're chasing down, but the one we keep coming back to is that the letter X serves as a symbol that perhaps your wife saw something that she either wasn't supposed to, or maybe she didn't realize that she wasn't supposed to see. And she paid the ultimate punishment. Do you have any thoughts on this?"

"N-no," he stutters, shifting in his seat. "No, I don't."

Kellan and I exchange glances.

Bingo.

TWENTY-FOUR

ROWAN

Kellan pushes off the wall where he'd been leaning and joins me at the table, though he stands while we remain sitting. He peers down at Zach and his attorney. An act of intimidation.

Zach is now fidgeting with the cufflink on his dress shirt. His attorney has noticed his client's shift in demeanor as well, and is sitting on the edge of his seat, ready to pull the plug on this interview.

"Mr. Kaing, I understand that you and your wife have been trying to get pregnant, but have had trouble doing so."

Zach's dark eyes pop. "How did you hear that?"

Simultaneously, Dennis says, "Detective, that's irrelevant. Zach, you don't need to answer this."

"No, it's okay," Zach frowns, eyes locked on me. "Where did you hear that?"

"Your neighbor, Amos Hoyt."

Dennis scribbles in his notebook.

Zach closes his eyes and blows out a breath. He shakes his head. "I told her—I *told* her that man was a gossip." He scrubs his palms over his face. "I can't believe she would tell *our neighbor* that."

"So it's true?"

"Yes." Zach raises his hand to cut off his lawyer, who was about to interject. "Alyssa has had two miscarriages, and we had trouble even getting pregnant in the first place."

"That must be difficult for you."

"Yes, and to be honest, it's causing—did cause—a lot of tension between us."

"Why?"

"Alyssa..." Zach glances at his attorney. "Alyssa hasn't always been a clean-living person. And I—well, I wonder if that's why she has had so much trouble getting pregnant."

She. It's always *she.* The woman has the trouble—not the man. It's always the woman's fault.

"Help me understand what you mean by clean-living," I ask.

Again, he looks at his attorney. Dennis nods, giving his client the approval.

Zach refocuses on me. "She was an addict."

"Drugs?"

"Yes."

"What kind?"

"Everything."

"Was she using at the time of her death?"

"No. God no. She's been sober—from drugs, anyway, for five years. She cleaned up right before we met. I drew a hard line in the sand that I would not accept anything less."

"Mr. Kaing..." I tilt my head to the side. "What was it that attracted you to Alyssa?"

Zach draws in a long inhale, and by the expression on his face, I can tell that this isn't the first time he's been asked this question, nor considered it himself.

"I met her at a bar. She was working three jobs to make ends meet. She was attractive and funny and we hit it off. I respected her work ethic and how she was trying to rebuild her life."

Like most macho men, Zach Kaing's kryptonite is a damsel in distress. I glance at Kellan, wondering if it's the same for him. And I'm the work-in-progress.

I refocus on Zach. "How were things between you two before you left, aside from the pregnancy issues?"

"Not great. To be honest, that's why I hadn't spoken to her since I left. We're not in a good spot. We got in a fight before I left—at dinner, the night before."

"What was the argument about?"

"Everything. It was one of those arguments that started small and escalated into bigger things. She wants to try fertility treatments, and I don't think I want to go that route." He pauses. "I just—I don't know if I want to do all that. It almost feels like the universe is telling us that we shouldn't have kids."

"Was she upset when you left?"

"I think so, yes."

"Did she try to reach out to you?"

"Yes, several times. I didn't respond."

Ice cold, indeed.

"Can you tell me about your neighbor? Amos Hoyt."

"I don't know much about him other than Alyssa befriended him."

"Have you met him?"

"I don't think so—if so, it was brief enough that I don't remember." He frowns. "Is he a suspect?"

"I can't get into those details with you. But do you know that she gave him a key to your home?"

"*What?*"

I nod. "Mr. Hoyt claims that she gave it to him, 'in case of an emergency.'"

It's obvious by his expression that Zach was unaware of this and that he is both surprised and angry at this news. His lawyer is feverishly scribbling in his notebook.

"Do you know what emergency she was referring to?"

"No. I have no idea. Geez, no."

"Did Alyssa ever say anything about someone following her?"

Again, he appears to be surprised. "No. No, not once."

Kellan and I share a glance.

"Mr. Hoyt told us that she told him that she felt like she was being followed in the weeks leading up to her death."

"What? No, she didn't say a thing. That doesn't make sense."

"Mr. Kaing, as you know, we searched the crime scene—your house—extensively but I was wondering if we could also have access to Alyssa's electronics, like her computer, or if you have a house computer, we'd like that too."

"I understand you are already working to obtain access to my client's wife's texts and call logs," Dennis injects.

"Yes, but I would like to dig deeper."

Zach is suddenly very still. My instincts scream at me.

"I don't think there is anything there that would help you with this," he says.

"Yes, but perhaps—"

"You'll need to get a warrant for that." His attorney stands. "This interview is done."

TWENTY-FIVE

ROWAN

I look up at the sound of fingers rapping against the office door.

"Open," I holler.

Kellan steps into my office, closing the door behind him.

I glance at the clock. It's eight-fifteen in the evening.

I blink and rub my eyes as Kellan crosses the room. My eyes sting, my mouth is dry, my stomach is empty. It's been a long day. After interviewing Zach Kaing, I met with the team for updates, and then had to re-shift my focus to the dozen other cases I'm working on—cases that I have neglected over the last forty-eight hours. The afternoon was filled with endless paperwork. I am drowning.

As Kellan removes a stack of papers from the seat across from my desk, I tap the face of my phone—no message from my husband asking if I'm okay or inquiring why I'm running late.

I blow out breath and lean back in my chair.

Kellan sinks into the chair across from me and crosses his leg over his knee. "Did you see the email?"

"What email?"

"Darcy just sent through the official autopsy report."

I sit up, click into my email.

"Here are the CliffsNotes: Alyssa died of asphyxia."

"So the killer strangled her to death—just like we thought."

"Right. And there is no DNA under her fingernails, no semen, not so much as a cuticle of hair that doesn't belong to her on her body."

"Dammit. No trace evidence from the assailant at all?"

"Nope. I think whoever did this knows what they're doing. Oh, and the mutilation was done after she was dead."

"So then it is unequivocally a message. The killer did not carve her eyes to torture her. It's a message—for us."

"I agree. And I agree with the assessment that Alyssa did something or saw something that she wasn't supposed to and she paid her life for it."

I begin chewing on the tip of my pen, a nasty habit I've had since college. "Kaing's hiding something."

"One hundred percent. He closed up like a clam when you mentioned the computers."

"I know. Makes me wanna get into his computer even more. I spoke with Chief Hood. We'd need a solid reason for the warrant, which we do not have—currently."

Kellan nods, sighs. He hates red tape as much as I do.

"They're an odd couple, Alyssa and Zach," I muse.

"Odd is subjective."

I roll my eyes, knowing he's referring to my husband and me. Kellan has made it clear that he thinks I have an odd relationship with Shepherd. He doesn't know the half of it.

A beat passes between us.

"You okay?" Kellan asks.

"I'm tired."

"I know but it seems more than that. Ever since the moment you showed up at the Kaings' house—"

"I'm tired, Kellan." I shut down my computer and push back from the chair.

"Where are you going?" Kellan stands as I do.

"I'm going for a jog."

"I'll join you."

"No."

"It's late, Rowan. It's not safe to jog after dark."

I snort. "Please."

Kellan grabs my arm as I round the desk. "Take Banjo if you won't take me."

"I planned on it."

"Why don't we go somewhere and get a quick bite to eat first?"

"No." I jerk out his hold. "Not tonight."

TWENTY-SIX

AMBER

I can't get the woman in the notebook out of my head. Her unnamed face has taken up residence between my ears and is screaming at me. What she's saying, however, is muddled somewhere between the past and present, a distant memory that is making me crazy.

I've tucked Connor into bed, fed my husband, and cleaned the kitchen. Mark is now watching sports in the living room, so loud that a bomb could hit our front yard and he wouldn't hear it, and I have escaped to the garage.

I slide my glass of wine onto one of the dusty shelves, careful to avoid the spider web in the corner. After kneeling next to the dozen boxes that contain all my old client files, I set the notebook on the floor and open to the page where my client felt like she was being watched.

"Okay, I'm listening," I said, like I'm talking to a damn Ouija board. "Guide me if you have something to tell me."

I pick a random client file, open, and filter through the contents. Definitely not my mystery writer. I scan another, then another.

File after file, I search for anything to help spark a solid memory, but get nothing other than a reminder of how damn hard life is, how many people struggle behind closed doors, behind perfect facades.

It's disheartening, and frankly, extremely depressing.

With a heavy sigh, I down the rest of my wine and lie down on the cold concrete where I stare at the ceiling until sleep takes me.

TWENTY-SEVEN

ROWAN

It is a moonless night, not a single star in the sky. Despite the chilled air, sweat drips down the side of my face. My heart is pounding, my legs are heavy, my stomach uneasy as I sprint over the pavement. The sidewalk is covered in slick, dead leaves, making it dangerous for running.

Unsurprisingly, I am alone on the jogging trail. The path ahead is illuminated only as far as the light of each lamp post will reach. Dangerous for a woman.

Seven, eight, nine, I count each post as I pass.

Banjo jogs beside me, tongue lolling, ears perched, having the time of his life. He was ecstatic when I stopped by the house to pick him up; unbeknownst to him, the real reason I stopped by was to ensure Shepherd was home and not out at the bar.

I slow as I pass post eleven, twelve, and then come to a full stop at post thirteen. Banjo circles my legs as I bend over to catch my breath, his leash tangling around my ankles. After a quick glance over my shoulder, I slip into the shadows of the woods, the dewy grass instantly saturating my tennis shoes.

I tap into the compass app on my watch and confirm that I am going southwest. Once I am certain I am out of the view of the trail, I click on my cell phone flashlight to guide the way. This part of the woods is overgrown, the brush thick and gnarled, cutting into my calves as I push through it. I am far away from the park now, deep into a section of woods that is rarely traveled.

I press on, my legs growing weaker. Eventually, the trees thin and the terrain becomes rocky. Large, craggy boulders spear up from the earth. I slow down as I near The Cliff, the place Kellan and I secretly meet. I pause behind a tree, and stare at the the the picnic tables where we share coffee, the swing where we share wine.

My stomach knots.

I step away from the tree and begin again, checking my compass to ensure I'm on the right path.

Banjo suddenly stops, lifts his nose and begins sniffing wildly. I shine the flashlight around, but can only see about a five-foot radius.

I unleash him. He bolts like a rocket. I take off after him, having to push into a sprint to keep up. The light bounces as I run, turning the woods into a dizzying discotheque.

His barks turn into manic yips.

I finally catch up to Banjo at the edge of a ravine. My heart hammers as I peer down into the abyss. Though the light from my cell phone hardly illuminates the space below, there is no mistaking the outline of the body laying at the bottom of the ravine.

"Shit..." I shove the phone in my pocket, thread my fingers together and grip the top of my head. "Shit, shit, shit. Okay, it's okay," I say to Banjo as much as to myself. We are both pacing now. "Everything's okay, buddy, everything's okay." I stroke his head while staring at the outline below. "Okay," I exhale, regaining composure. "I need you to stay here, buddy, okay?"

After re-clipping Banjo to his leash and then attaching the

leash to a tree, I position my phone in my waistband—keeping the flashlight on—and slowly climb down the edge of the ravine.

The moment my shoes reach the bottom, I spin around, retrieve my phone, and shine the light.

The body is on its side, wedged between two sharp rocks, and is obviously dead. It's a woman, based on the long brown hair and feminine clothing. She is wearing a pair of blue jeans, a gray sweater, and slip-on ballet flats, though one has fallen off. The back of her head dangles over the edge of the rock, her feet off the other edge. I immediately note the lack of blood around the body. This woman was not killed here.

Carefully, I cross the ravine, shining the torch along her body as I maneuver around the rock.

The side of the woman's face is crushed from either the fall over the ravine or a blunt instrument. Flies and bugs swarm in and out of the oozing tissues.

My stomach lurches and I cover my nose and mouth.

The woman's arm is dangling outward, as if reaching for me, and carved into the skin of her palm is the letter X.

TWENTY-EIGHT

ROWAN

Twenty-five years earlier

Mascara-colored tears streamed down my cheeks as I pressed the blade to my wrist. You'll have to press hard, *I reminded myself, trying to control the tremor in my hand. I'd practiced on oranges —six of them, actually. I knew that lots of pressure and a swift back-and-forth sawing motion was the only way to break through the skin. I knew it would hurt, but I also knew that once it was over, I'd never have to hurt again.*

It was time. I'd never been surer of anything in my life. I was ready to leave the earth, plain and simple. I didn't want this life, one filled with children's shelters and foster homes, and I didn't see a light at the end of the tunnel. Hell, I couldn't even see the end of the tunnel, and maybe that was the worst.

My reason for no longer wanting to be here had nothing to do with addiction, betrayal, grief, debt, or anything like that. It was because I had simply given up. I had no hope. And a world without hope is a very, very dark place.

I was in my bathroom at the shelter, sitting cross-legged in the bathtub. I'd chosen that spot because I didn't want to make a big, bloody mess for the staff to clean up. Weeks earlier, I'd stolen scissors from the rec room, although I'd been contemplating ending my life for months before that.

I looked at the roadmap of veins on my inner wrist. I reminded myself to cut along the vein, not across it, so that I'd die quicker. I'd read that somewhere.

I'd already vomited twice in the toilet, and now, my heart was pounding so hard I could actually see it pumping through my veins.

I focused on a plume of mold in the corner of the bathtub. I stared at that nasty black spot for what seemed like eternity. Slowly, my pulse slowed and a wave of calm came over. A feeling of peace, almost like happiness, because I realized that I would never, ever, have to feel this way again.

The initial puncture felt like a bee sting, a zip of pain from the top of my head to the tip of my toes. But the sawing—the severing of the skin—was almost unbearable. Like someone had lit fire to my entire body.

That was when Shepherd came in. The boy I'd spent almost every day with since meeting years earlier. The boy I'd lost my virginity to. The boy who the others warned me to stay away from, the boy rumored to have "serious issues." Which, let's be honest, only made me want him more. Because I, too, had serious issues.

That was the day Shepherd saved my life.

The day he took my heart for his own.

TWENTY-NINE

ROWAN

"Her name is Macy Swift, do you know her?" Sergeant Chris Hoffman asks Kellan and me as we stare down at the body. Hoffman was the first to arrive on scene, Kellan shortly after, followed by Darcy, the medical examiner.

Kellan and I shake our heads in unison.

"She's married to a local real estate developer; Jerry Swift is his name. They own an excavation company. Lots of money."

Kellan nods. "I'm vaguely familiar with the name."

"How do you know them?" I ask Chris.

"She goes to my gym. She does a lot of philanthropy stuff. Runs a few charities."

"Are you two friendly?"

"No, I just recognize her."

"So we've got another rich stay-at-home wife whose body is carved with the letter X," Darcy mutters, hovering over the body with a magnifying glass. The scene is illuminated with flashlights that both Kellan and Hoffman carried down from their vehicles. Soon, the scene will be lit up with Klieg lights and crawling with crime scene techs.

Two deaths in only a few days just kicked things up a notch.

"How long do you think she's been dead?" Hoffman asks.

"Less than twenty-four hours," Darcy responds. "Right around there, probably. My guess is that she was killed about this time last night. I can tell most of the contusions are post-mortem, so I'm assuming she was dumped here after she was killed. And, based on the marks around her neck, I'm also guessing she was strangled, just like Alyssa Kaing."

"If someone dumped her, then there has to be tracks from whoever did it." Hoffman looks at me. "Did you check for boot prints?"

"Yes. There were none."

"Then whoever did this must have covered their tracks." Kellan rubs his chin. "I'm telling you, we are dealing with someone who knows what they're doing."

Hoffman shakes his head. "There's got to be tracks some-where. Or drag marks at least. Whoever dumped her had to have either carried or dragged her. There's no way somebody could get an ATV or a four-wheeler through this brush."

"It's ballsy," I muse, "carrying a dead body through the woods."

"Or reckless," Kellan adds.

"Or is it exactly what the killer intends?" Hoffman says, this earning our full attention.

"What do you mean?"

"Well, we established that the manner in which Alyssa Kaing was killed was emotional. Someone had a beef with her." He nods to the body on the ground. "This woman's hands are carved with the same symbol. If Alyssa *saw* something she wasn't supposed to, then this woman *did* something she wasn't supposed to. Touched, held—did."

A moment of silence lingers as we consider this.

Hoffman continues, "I'm saying that whoever is killing these women wants the bodies to be seen. They want the messages to be connected. They don't care about getting caught carrying a dead body through the woods because to them, the message is what is most important." He fists his hands on his hips and looks around. "Why this location, I wonder? How did you find the body?"

"I was jogging with Banjo, off the leash, when suddenly he just took off into the woods." As if on cue, Banjo whines from the tree he's tied to a few yards away. "I lost him for a good ten minutes before finding him at the edge of the ravine."

After a pause, Hoffman dips his chin. "Okay. I'm going to search around the scene. You guys good?"

Kellan and I nod.

"I think he's onto something," Kellan says as Chris's flashlight fades into the darkness. "Whoever is doing this wants us to know why."

"Why?"

"They want the sins of these women to be revealed. Whatever these two women did are bad enough to die for—in the killer's eyes, at least. And they want us to figure it out. I'm guessing this is someone who likes the game, the chase."

"Agreed. It's definitely someone with an ego. Hey, Darcy?" The medical examiner looks over her shoulder. "When can you get this autopsy done?"

"Same as with Alyssa; as soon as I can."

"I want you to call me immediately—no matter day or night."

"You got it." Darcy pauses. "Allyssa's husband is back in town, right?"

"Yes. But he didn't land until this afternoon. If this woman was killed last night, Zach Kaing is officially *off* our suspect list."

"Somebody needs to go to the trailhead," Kellan says, glancing at the phone beeping on his hip. "The techs will be here any minute, and so will the media."

"I'll do it."

My phone rings. I step aside and pull it from my pocket, noticing my hand is trembling.

"Velky," I answer.

"Detective, hey, it's Willa from dispatch, up here at the station."

"What's going on?"

"Zach Kaing just showed up here; says he needs to talk to you."

"Now?"

"Yeah."

Kellan walks up behind me, eavesdropping.

"I'll be right there."

"FYI," Willa says. "I'm pretty sure he's drunk. If not, he's a total mess. Just wanted to give you a heads up."

"Thanks."

I shove my phone into my pocket. "I've got to go. Zach just showed up at the station, says he wants to talk."

"I'm coming with you."

"*No*. Stay here. They need someone—"

"No—"

"Detective Palmer, stay here at the scene. That's an order."

THIRTY

ROWAN

Zach Kaing surges off his chair as I step through the police station sliding glass doors. Willa wasn't joking. The guy's a mess. His eyes are bloodshot, his face flushed and riddled with nerves. He's wearing a T-shirt with the beginnings of sweat stains under the arms, a pair of baggy basketball shorts, and running shoes that are untied. A far cry from the expensive suit he was wearing for our meeting earlier in the day. I notice that his attorney, Dennis, is not with him.

"Detective." He rushes to me, and on instinct, my body flinches.

"Mr. Kaing, is everything alright?" I ask, taking a step back.

"I need to talk to you."

This is when I notice what appears to be a laptop sleeve clutched to his chest.

"Okay, let me get the conference room ready. I'll be right back, please wait here."

Willa is watching, wide-eyed from behind the bullet-proof glass as I swipe my badge and slip through the door. I poke my head around the corner. "You weren't kidding. He's a mess. Did he come alone?"

"I think so, yes."

"Check the security cameras outside and confirm that please."

"Will do."

"Has he made any calls since he's been waiting?"

"No."

"Texts? On his phone at all?"

"No, he's been pacing like a wild animal. I've kept my eye on him. Don't worry."

"Good, thank you. You did the right thing by calling me. No matter what time of day or night, if it's my case, always call."

"Yes ma'am."

I begin to turn away, but pause. "Hey, if we're back there for a while, will you poke your head outside and make sure Banjo's okay? He's in my car; I left the windows cracked."

"Of course."

"Thanks. And if Shepherd calls, tell him I'm in an unexpected meeting. I'm going to put my cell on silent."

"You got it."

I hurry back to the conference room to ensure the table is clean of any paperwork that might have been left behind from previous meetings. Then I rush to the break room and start a pot of coffee. I think we are both going to need it.

When I return to the lobby, Zach is standing in front of the window, gripping the computer like a newborn baby.

"You ready?"

He startles, turns, then follows me into the station.

"We'll be in the same room we were in earlier today." I gesture him inside where he takes a seat in the same chair he'd chosen hours earlier. He slides the computer onto the table.

"Can I get you some coffee before we begin?"

"No. God no. I've had... I don't know how many pots today."

"Okay," I pause, look him over. "Where's Dennis, your attorney?"

"I didn't call him."

"Are you sure that's a wise decision?"

"Yes. I don't care. I don't... I have to get this off my chest."

"Okay then." I slide into the chair across from him, open up my notebook, and click my pen. "What's going on?"

"I have something to tell you." Zach drags in a shaky breath. "Before Alyssa and I met, she was with this guy for a few years. She actually dumped him to be with me."

"Who?"

"His name is Travis McCain."

I jot down the name.

"He's in jail now. I checked. Got arrested for his third DWI."

"What jail?"

"Houston Central."

"How long as he been there?"

"Two weeks, the guy I spoke to said."

So I can immediately cross him off the suspect list.

"Anyway..." Zach jabs his fingers through his hair, leaving a mess of tangles standing on end. "He had a child, a little girl. One night, when Alyssa had too much to drink, she told me that he was abusive to both her and his child."

"What kind of abuse?"

"Physical. But I guess it got pretty bad with the little girl."

"Did Alyssa tell anyone?"

"No, and she felt horribly guilty for that. Back then she was using pretty heavy. But after she cleaned up, she really regretted not turning him in. It ate at her, you know?"

"Why didn't she turn him in, ever? She could have called the police even years later, requesting a welfare visit?"

Zach looks down. "I asked her not to. I didn't want to get

involved with any of it. I told her it wasn't our business anymore."

"Okay... so what does this have to do with the computer you're holding?"

"This is her computer. There are emails between her and him on it from a few months back. When he found out she and I were married and that we had money, he tried to blackmail Alyssa, saying that he would tell her husband, me, that she abused his girl and that's why he ended it. There's even a picture of the little girl with a black eye. He sent it to mess with Alyssa. It's awful."

"What was his blackmail request?"

"Ten thousand dollars, and before you ask, yes, I paid it. I paid him to stay out of our lives and I threatened him physically if he came back."

"I see."

"That's not all." Zach scrubs his hands over his face, leaving angry red marks on his cheeks. "Oh my God, I can't believe this."

"Zach, you came here to get this off your chest. The sooner you say it, the sooner it's done."

"The—the little girl died. The newspaper said it was an accident. She died not long after I wired him the money."

"And you don't think it was an accident?"

"No. I think he killed her. We talked about going to the police but I didn't want to be involved in any way with this mess, whatsoever. Alyssa has—had—my last name, and I just don't... I have business to protect." He pushes the computer sleeve in my direction. "That's her computer. All the emails are in there. Like I said, her ex is in jail so there's no way he killed her, but the timing just seems like such a coincidence, you know? It feels like it has to be connected somehow."

"Do you think that her ex could have been the person who was following her? Assuming someone was."

"I think that makes sense. I also think that's why she gave our neighbor a key to the home. I'm gone a lot, and I think she was worried Travis would find out where we lived and come by. I think... she was scared about that and wanted someone she trusted to have access to our home in case something happened to her."

"That's explains a lot."

He nods. "Anyway, I don't know the password to her computer, but I'm sure your tech guys can figure it out pretty quickly."

"Thank you, Zach. You did the right thing. I need you to fill out some paperwork that basically says you're consenting to release this into evidence."

"Fine. Yes. I'll do whatever I need to. I don't ever want to see that computer again." He releases a long exhale, the relief of a confession. How wonderful it must feel.

He leans in, his eyes sad. "So do you think all this has something to do with her death?"

"To be determined," I say. But in my gut I know this has everything to do with his wife's murder. The message is loud and clear. Alyssa turned a blind eye to child abuse, and she lost her eyes because of it.

A dozen new questions swarm my head.

Aside from Zach and Travis, who knew these intimate details of Alyssa's personal life? And how?

THIRTY-ONE

ROWAN

"So both murders are definitely connected and we've got a vigilante killer—some idiot taking justice into their own hands and punishing these women how they see fit." Kellan scrubs his hands over his face. He hasn't stopped pacing the conference room since we arrived.

It's eleven o'clock in the morning. The team—Evelyn, Chris, Kellan and myself—is assembled, and the tension in the room is so thick you could cut a knife through it. The news of another woman found murdered has rocked the small town of Blackbird Cove. The phones are ringing off the hook, tips coming in by the second. Multiple media vans clog the parking lot, and the gossip and conspiracy theories are running rampant. The citizens are scared and demanding answers.

Chief Hood has joined via video call. Despite being on a beach vacation with his family, the chief is looking as sharp as ever, wearing a pressed collared shirt. Even his trademark side part is perfectly combed, not a strand out of place. His presence has only added to my anxiety. The discovery of a second body means the chief will have his nose in every move I make from this moment on.

I begin my update, informing everyone of Zach Kaing's late-night confession about his wife's abusive ex, the blackmail, and the passing of the ex's child, which was ruled accidental.

"I verified that Alyssa's ex, Travis McCain, was in jail at the time of both murders, so it's physically impossible that he killed both women. Also, after speaking with him over the phone, I don't get the vibe that he paid someone to do it. One, because he appeared to have no clue who Macy Swift was—so why would he want to kill her—and two, this guy's sole motivations in life are money and drugs. Paying someone to kill Alyssa isn't in his interest. In fact, the opposite is, so that he could continue to blackmail her."

"So are we even considering him a suspect?"

"No. I don't want to waste our time or resources on him. Does everyone agree?"

Nods around the table.

"Okay, switch gears. This is what we currently know about victim number two." I gesture to the projector where an image of Macy Swift fills the screen. In this picture pulled from social media, she is sitting in a lawn chair, wine glass in one hand, cell phone in the other, and a smile as wide as Texas across her face. "Macy Swift is a thirty-one-year-old stay at home wife who is married to Jerry Swift, a wealthy real estate developer. She and her husband have several homes across the country. When I spoke with Jerry just a bit ago, he informed me that, four days ago, Macy told her husband that she felt like she was being followed. We know that Alyssa Kaing also reported that she felt like someone was following her."

"But we don't know anything more about this mystery person other than he or she was following the women, right?" the Chief asks. "Not even height, weight, ethnicity?"

"Right."

He shakes his head. "Unbelievable."

I click to another image, a grainy black and white of a

woman crossing a street. "The last time Macy Swift was seen alive was on this street camera while on her way to Blackbird Trail for a jog. This is her in the picture. She was never seen or heard from again until I discovered her body. It is estimated she was killed anywhere from three to six hours after being recorded on this camera.

"Here's where things get interesting. We've learned that Macy Swift lives a double life—one that we now know has been under surveillance by the FBI. During the day, Macy ran a charity for sick children with rare genetic diseases. During the night, she spent every penny received by that charity on hand-bags, designer clothing, vacations, and jewelry. According to the FBI, Macy has embezzled over two hundred thousand dollars from her charity over the last five years. They suspect the husband's contracting business is dirty as well, which is why they haven't arrested Macy yet."

"Holy crap," Evelyn gaffs.

I glance at the clock. "In two hours, we have a meeting with two FBI agents, who are currently driving up from the Houston office"—I glance at my notes—"Special Agent Brian Briggs, and Special Agent Jacob Zeal. They will likely inform us that they are going to take over the case—both Alyssa Kaing's and Macy Swift's, considering it appears both cases are connected. I've called this internal meeting for us to compare notes and align on exactly what and how we want to update the FBI. Questions?"

When no one responds, I continue.

"So. We are all on the same page that the X's carved into Macy's palms are a message, just like the X's carved into Alyssa's eyes. In Alyssa's case, she turned a blind eye to child abuse, in Macy's case she stole money from sick kids—eyes, hands. The killer, whoever it is, is punishing these women for their sins and wants everyone to know about them. Is everyone on the same page with this?"

Nods across the room.

Kellan stops mid-pace, flicks his finger into the air. "We need to understand if there is a connection between the victims. Macy's husband said he didn't think she and Alyssa were friends, or even knew each other at all, and neither follow each other on social media. But there's got to be something. How would the killer know both of their dirty secrets?"

"What about Amos Hoyt?" Hoffman says. "He obviously knew Alyssa well, I wonder if he has any connection to Macy Swift, too?"

Evelyn taps her pen. "Ah, that reminds me. My nurse friend got back to me—Hoyt's medical file is relatively normal. No dementia, nothing weird, certainly nothing that would negate his testimony of what happened. He has a prescription for medical marijuana to help with his PTSD from his time in the military, so the joints you saw at his house are legit. And of course, if this information goes beyond this room, my friend will get fired and I will be extremely upset. Please don't make me upset today."

"No one wants to see that, trust me." I wink. "Okay, thanks. I'll pay Hoyt another visit," I say, scribbling in my notebook. "To see if Alyssa ever mentioned Macy, or if he knows her as well."

I lean back and chew on my pen. "But it doesn't feel like the women knowing each other is part of this. It seems like the sin that these women were committing is the motive, *not* the actual women themselves. I think the killer somehow uncovered these women's secrets and wants the world to know what they did."

Hoffman nods. "I agree, but we need to know *how* the killer knew these women's secrets."

"I think we need to consider the child angle," Kellan offers.

"What do you mean?"

"Alyssa turned a blind eye to child abuse, and Macy was stealing from a child charity. Kids—*that's* a connection. And we've already established that it appears that the murders are emotional. Kids make people emotional."

"So the killer has a soft spot for children?" Evelyn tilts her head to the side, skeptical. "If that's true, and the killer's motive is to kill everyone who has wronged children, then his list is quite literally endless." She leans forward, twirling a pink pen through her acrylics. "Also, if that is the case, why not just come to us about it? The police?"

"Unless it *is* one of us," Hoffman mutters, cocking a brow.

"Keep that shit to yourself, to be clear," Chief Hood barks into the camera. "That is not something we want to mention when meeting with the FBI. We do *not* need that heat right now."

Kellan turns toward the camera and addresses the chief in the cool yet commanding demeanor that I have grown to both respect and envy about him. "I agree that we shouldn't tell the FBI, but I do agree with Chris. Think about it for a second: In Alyssa's case, we know that there was no struggle before she was killed, therefore we know that she either knew her assailant, or that it was someone she trusted—like someone in a uniform. It's the same with Macy's case. The medical examiner said there were no signs of struggle, meaning Macy also felt comfortable with whoever approached her on the trail. And, also, there is not a single fucking piece of trace evidence at either scene. The killer knows what they're doing—I'm telling you, we cannot ignore this angle."

"It's way too early to count out trace evidence, Kellan," I say. "We haven't even been back to Macy's dump site."

"What about a copycat killer?" Hoffman asks.

I shake my head. "It's only been a couple days since Alyssa's body was found. I don't think the story has had enough time to grow legs to entice a copycat killer."

"So basically," Chief Hood interrupts, clearly impatient. "We have no concrete suspect, and jack shit to tell the FBI."

I clear my throat. "Correct, sir. Our current leads are based on interviews, not tangible evidence."

I steel myself for the rant that follows.

My head is throbbing as I pull out of the station parking lot.

After a quick glance in the rearview mirror, I pluck my cell phone from the cup holder and call the senior facility to ensure Aunt Jenny is there, and not at home. Then, I take a detour to the gym, and ensure Shepherd is there.

Then, I hurry home.

THIRTY-TWO

ROWAN

My hands shake as I pull the clothes from the hamper. Cradling the pieces like a newborn baby, I jog to the living room and dump them in the middle of the floor. Banjo whines from the other side of sliding glass door, but I don't pay him any attention. The sound barely even registers.

I run to the garage, grab a bottle of lighter fluid and a lighter.

My blood roars in my ears as I shove the clothes into the fireplace and carefully douse each piece with lighter fluid. My hands are trembling so badly that it takes four tries to ignite the lighter.

I sink back on my haunches as the flames ignite.

Fifteen minutes later, I wipe the tears from my face, scoop the ashes into a metal trashcan, pull on a baseball cap, and drive to Piper's Pier.

THIRTY-THREE

Personal Notes—Dictated

Special Agent Darla Thatcher, PhD
Case 927-4 "RS"

I am becoming very concerned about RS. Perhaps I should start by saying I am guilty of allowing our relationship to go beyond the traditional agent/victim relationship. I take full responsibility for this error. However, it's important to note that this happened because RS insists on only meeting with me, he will only speak with me, and continues to request meetings beyond what is expected or needed, especially at this point in the case. I allowed this, under the circumstances. However, with each new meeting, RS exhibits new and alarming behavior and I am becoming increasingly concerned about his mental state.

Per his medical documents, RS has recently been diagnosed with ADHD (along with PTSD, which was diagnosed almost immediately). However, I fear this latest diagnosis is incorrect. I believe it is much more than that.

RS has self-harmed twice now, both in response to what he perceived as failure on his part. For example, we tried art therapy. RS hated his painting so much that he threw it across the room, cracking the window, then proceeded to pick up the easel and bash it against the floor until it broke into several pieces. This outburst was in response to the art therapist suggesting he do something different than he was doing. RS took this as criticism. Later, he cut himself with a dull butterknife. He was punishing himself, I believe, for "failing" the therapist. This, along with a similar instance, shows a significant increase in lack of self-control, inappropriate emotion, hostility, and a skewed sense of self (i.e., everything he does is bad—he has told me this verbatim).

RS is also showing alarming paranoia. He is having trouble sleeping. The doors and windows must be locked, the shades drawn, and overhead light must be on. Even then, I don't think he sleeps, though I cannot prove this.

I strongly believe RS needs a multi-day psychiatric evaluation in addition to the therapy that is already being provided. Pharmaceutical intervention must be considered at this point.

This is beyond the scope of my job as well as expertise. Combining this with unnatural attachment RS has formed to me, I have made the difficult decision to request that another agent take over his case.

THIRTY-FOUR

AMBER

Something is going on with Rowan. For one, she showed up twenty minutes early for our 5 p.m. session, and Rowan is never early. And two, she looks like she's been run over by a truck. It's not just the messy hair, the dark circles, and sallow skin; it's the wild look in her eye. Behind the exhaustion is a madness that I've seen before in my clients, usually right before a mental break.

This concerns me. What has happened between our last meeting and now?

I lean back and take her in. She's staring out the window, shredding her cuticles. I can practically hear her thoughts spinning. Her trademark blue button-up is dirty with what appears to be ash, her slacks wrinkled. Her shoes are speckled with fresh mud, as if she's just come from a hike.

I follow her gaze out the window. Two squirrels bicker violently at the base of a tree, then skirt up the trunk and disappear into the shadows of the brown, brittle leaves. It is a cool, overcast autumn day. Dreary and bleak, with rain in the forecast. Dark, just like Rowan's mood.

Five minutes pass, ten. My eyes never leave her, not once. This complex enigma of a woman.

At the fifteen-minute mark, I speak.

"How's work?"

"In general? Or are you referring to the two dead women found recently?"

Minimal details of both murders have been leaked and are already threaded through dozens of conspiracy theories. There is no longer need for prudence on Rowan's part.

"Both," I respond.

"I wouldn't know anymore," she scowls. "The FBI took over both cases this afternoon."

"Really?"

"Yes, it's not uncommon for the local office to step in with a possible serial killer scenario, especially if there is media coverage. But, aside from that, one of the women was already on their radar, so naturally, they pounced."

"I heard the ways in which the women were killed were similar."

Rowan doesn't respond, which is answer enough.

"Does this lessen your workload? Last time we met, you mentioned how busy you were."

"Not really. Now I'm playing catch up with the other cases I neglected while working that one."

I watch as Rowan pulls a cuticle, creating a line of blood next to her nail. I wince. She doesn't even seem to feel the pain.

I clear my throat. "You're handling a lot. All the time, Rowan. And on that note, I'd like to revisit how our last appointment ended. Specifically, that you think Shepherd is cheating on you."

"He is." Rowan finally looks at me.

"How do you know for certain?"

"He has a new tattoo on his wrist, hidden under the watch he always wears."

"What is it?"

"I didn't recognize it at first, but it is the symbol for Zhiva."

"Who's Zhiva?"

"A goddess in Slavic mythology."

"Ah, I remember you telling me that Shepherd is of Russian descent. Velky is a Russian name, right?"

"Yes," she says, "Shepherd's lineage is Russian, and he's proud of his roots. He has like, ten books on the history of Russia."

"What does the symbol mean?"

"Love."

My brows pop. "Really?"

"Specifically, love and fertility."

"And you think this new tattoo serves as a symbol of his love for someone else?"

"He wouldn't get a tattoo symbolizing love without it representing something. And it certainly has nothing to do with me." She looks out the window. "It is a sign of commitment to her." She swallows deeply. "And the fertility thing..."

"The fertility thing, what?"

"Shepherd has always wanted to have children."

"Yes, you've told me that. But you never told me why *you* don't want to have children."

She looks away.

"Rowan..."

"Because I'm worried I'm not cut out for motherhood."

"Why do you say that?"

"I didn't have the best example of a normal family growing up. And Shepherd, well, honestly? Sometimes it feels like somewhere along the timeline, our relationship has morphed from a romantic one to one where I am a mother to him. I don't know if I could handle throwing a baby into the mix—or how he would handle it. I would be raising two kids, so to speak."

"Twenty-four-seven is pretty constant. Maybe you need to release control a bit."

"No. I can't."

"Why?"

"He needs me." She pauses. "And a baby would need me. I worry that I can't do both."

"Well, it's also okay not to want children."

"Is it?"

"Absolutely."

"That's not what society says. Women are built for child-birth. Everyone has children."

"And everyone is miserable." I wink, though immediately feel guilty. An uncouth comment from a mother who recently discovered her child has unnamed cognitive issues. I glance at the clock, wondering if Connor is with Mark or Mark's mom. Last I'd checked she'd taken him somewhere in town. I should have asked where. Guilt twists in my stomach.

Rowan takes a deep breath. "I can see Shepherd being attracted to a woman who loves kids, or is young enough to bear his own."

"Seeing it doesn't make it so."

Rowan nods, glances down.

"You said 'her' as though you know who it is. Do you know who your husband is possibly having an affair with?"

"Not yet."

"Are you actively looking for her? Trying to figure out who she is?"

Rowan doesn't respond.

"Have you asked Shepherd point blank if he's having an affair?"

"No."

"Why?"

No response.

A minute passes.

"Rowan, you have a serious mental block when it comes to your husband and marriage. Why?"

No response.

"If you remember, I've previously said that I believe there is something in your past that is responsible for you holding back. Something that makes you feel like you need the security that marriage offers, despite the fact yours seems to be falling apart. Can we talk about this, please?"

She shifts, but doesn't say no.

We need to talk about this, Rowan." I pause. "When you first began coming to me, it was in your medical file that you spent most of your childhood in child services. Do you mind if I ask you some questions about this?"

Her body visibly stiffens. A moment later, she nods.

"Thank you. We'll start slowly, okay? What did your mom do for work?"

"My mother was a waitress at the local waffle house. My dad was a drug dealer."

"When did you find out he was a drug dealer?"

"After I'd already been taken away—about a year into foster care. My schoolmates told me—they'd heard from their parents."

"That must have been difficult."

"Yes, my nickname in school was Rollin' Rowan. Ecstasy was having a moment back then."

"Kids are brutal."

"So are parents."

"What age did you go into foster care?"

"I was eleven years old. They finally took me after the sixth —the *sixth*—visit from CPS." She shakes her head, the emotion boiling underneath the surface. "Do you know how hard it is for a child to be taken away from their family? How dire the situation must be? It's an incredibly flawed system. I should have been taken away on their first visit, I know that now." Her eyes narrow with anger. "My parents started leaving me at school in *kindergarten*."

"What do you mean *leaving* you at school?"

"Exactly that. My parents wouldn't pick me up from school. They'd just drop me off and never come back. The school repeatedly tried to contact my parents for them to sign me up for the bus route, but they ignored the calls. It happened so many times that one of the teachers changed her schedule so that she could take me home. Mrs. Young. I'll never forget her... Looking back, I honestly think my parents were hoping that I would just never come home, that I'd find someone else to live with. That someone else would take me. They truly, truly, simply didn't want me."

"That must've been awful."

"Yeah, honestly it was. I remember being embarrassed more than anything else, because obviously the kids saw, and all the teachers knew. I'd start getting crippling anxiety around the end of the school day, anticipating how I'd get home. I'd get so nervous I'd have to go to the bathroom several times, and of course, that in itself was embarrassing." She shrugs. "Anyway, finally, with all the complaints, CPS took me away." She picks at another nail. "It's amazing how long they will let a child stay in an abusive environment."

"All the while, the emotional and mental damage is getting worse and worse."

"Exactly."

"Rowan, is this why you chose a job in law enforcement?"

"Yes. I wanted to try to fix a flawed system."

"Makes perfect sense. Tell me about life inside your home. Were you abused, aside from mentally?"

"No."

"Not physically?"

"No."

"Sexually?"

"No. I was just... cast aside. I was nothing to them. A burden, an annoying house gnat that you can't get rid of. I made my own food from a very young age, was left alone many nights, learned how to bathe myself, everything on my own."

"Rowan, do you think this is why you are so loyal to those in your life who have taken care of you?"

She frowns.

"Think about Aunt Jenny," I say. "You've taken her in, despite the hardship on both you and Shepherd. Now, think about your marriage. You're loyal to Shepherd because he made the ultimate commitment to you by marrying you. A commitment to never leave you or abandon you... at school, if you will. Do you see what I'm saying?

"Rowan, you have significant trauma that you have tucked away and compartmentalized—and I have a feeling that I don't even know the half of it. But what you may not realize is that these unaddressed events are ruling your life. For example, it is solely because of your traumatic childhood that you chose your career. That's big, right? Think about it. And because of your family abandoning you, you are clinging onto your husband, because, whether he's a crappy husband or not, he offers stability in your life. And also you feel a sense of loyalty toward him." I pause. "Your trauma as a child is why you need stability —no matter what the cost—and why you are loyal to a fault."

She's quiet now, still, the way she gets when she wants to stop talking.

"Rowan, if you want anything in your life to change, whether strengthening your marriage or having the courage to leave it, we have *got* to spend time unpacking your childhood. By doing this you'll begin to recognize the conditioned behavior you have as a result of the trauma. Meaning, decisions you have made even as an adult that are rooted in your childhood trauma —and you don't even realize it. Then, we'll work on rewiring how you interpret your traumatic events. Once we do all that, you'll begin to think more clearly and see things in a new light. It's incredibly emboldening, Rowan. Perhaps enough that you will finally be brave enough to leave your husband, if that is truly what you want when we get to that point."

"How long does all this take?" she asks quickly and sharply enough that it catches me off guard.

"It depends on how much work you're willing to do on your end."

She sighs, looks away.

I frown, lean forward. "Rowan is there a reason you're wanting to rush this?"

The detective pauses, then stares me straight in the eye. "That's an entirely different level of trauma that we will have to unpack one day."

Just then, my cell phone vibrates on the desk. I glance at the screen where a text from Emma pops up:

Emma: I need to talk.

THIRTY-FIVE

ROWAN

I never thought I'd be the woman who spies on her husband. In fact, I *loathe* that kind of woman. Yet here I am, hiding in the back of a parking lot, headlights off, parked between two massive Duallies with American flags hanging from the back windows. Last Call is crowded tonight. The bass from inside thrums through the window I'd cracked open. Sprinkles of rain sneak in, splattering on my forearm.

I've been here for an hour and forty-seven minutes, arriving exactly ten minutes after my husband, who unsurprisingly, was totally oblivious to the fact that he was being followed.

I watch a trio of rowdy cowboys push their way out the front doors. The music blasts through a puff of smoke that rolls out with them. I shake my head. It astonishes me that people still smoke cigarettes.

Next to them, a two-door baby-blue Smart Fortwo, the size of a matchbox car, squeaks into the parking lot. It also astonishes me that people actually buy these tiny cars. Coffins on wheels, I call them.

I watch a tall, thin, bleached-blonde in a mini skirt and cowboy boots duck out of the car. After checking her lipstick in the side mirror, she saunters across the parking lot. I envy that kind of confidence, the kind I've never had.

The kind my husband desires.

My attention is pulled to my phone, beeping in the console. I click the screen.

Kellan: We got Alyssa's credit card statements

Me: So?

Kellan: What do you mean so

Me: We're off the case

Kellan: We're not off, you've walked away from it. The feds might have taken lead but they want to work with us.

Me: Bullshit

Kellan: They need us. They don't know the area like we do.

Kellan: What the hell is going on with you?

Me: Nothing. What do the statements say? Anything interesting?

Kellan: Some fed kid is going through them now.

Me: What's a fed kid

Kellan: Some Gen-Z'er who smells like patchouli. I don't even think she's legal to drink.

Me: I have a feeling you'll find out soon enough

Kellan: No, I only have eyes for emotionally unavailable women who wear masculine dress shirts

Kellan: I was joking

Kellan: Meet me

Me: No

Kellan: Where are you?

Kellan: Ro. What's going on?

Kellan: Damn you Rowan

A tidal wave of emotion rolls over me. I turn off my phone and throw it in the cup holder.

Just then, a Jeep pulls into the parking lot—far too fast—and parks next to my husband's truck.

I sit up.

A woman—another blonde—climbs out of the Jeep. There's something familiar about her. Squinting, I lean forward, and watch as she settles a beaded purse over her shoulder. She reminds me of a fairy, tall, lithe, with a pixie face.

Then it hits me—Emma something. I recognize her from a picture Amber has in her clinic office. The picture stood out to me because it surprised me that Amber would be so reckless as to have personal photographs in an office where mentally unstable—let's just call it what it is—clients spend hours every day.

My instinct piques as I watch the beautiful woman breeze across the parking lot and step into the bar.

I wait, staring at the door, looking in the rearview mirror every few seconds, waiting—hoping—for a car of her teacher friends to pull up. It doesn't happen.

Emma is meeting someone at the bar. I wonder if that someone is my husband.

My stomach swirls and my eyes never leave the door.

Couples come and go, drunk, high, happy, laughing. None of whom are my husband, or Emma.

I grab my phone, and ignoring the texts from Kellan, run the license plate of the Jeep and learn Emma's last name is Thompson. Then, I click into social media and search until I find her page. I scroll through.

Emma in a beautiful pink dress.

Emma reading in bed.

Emma cooking in the kitchen.

Emma at the beach.

Emma in an airplane.

Emma in a bathing suit.

Emma: beautiful, young, fertile, skinny, happy.

"Fucking bitch," my voice shakes.

Tears well in my eyes.

With a guttural scream, I throw the phone against the windshield, drop my head into my hands, and begin to cry.

THIRTY-SIX

ROWAN

Thirteen years earlier

Grinning, I tugged at the blindfold covering my eyes. A dirty red bandana that smelled just like him.

"You know I hate surprises," I said as the truck bumped over a pothole, bouncing me into the air. I considered using the opportunity to "accidentally" remove the blindfold, but decided against it, a little voice in my head saying: let him have his moment.

It was early spring, at dusk. The time of day when the world is washed in an apricot golden glow. We were on a dirt road. The windows were down and I can still remember how fragrant the air was that day. Fresh, floral, earthy. Classic country music— Shepherd's favorite—played low on the radio. Shepherd's hand covered mine on the console, two beers sat in the cupholder between us.

After what seemed like an eternity, the truck came to a stop. The engine cut and the sounds of deep forest engulfed me.

"Let's see..." I said with a flourish and an English accent, "by

the sound of the water lapping lazily against the shore in the distance, I can deduct that we have arrived at Blackbird Lake."

"Nice work Detective Rowan," Shepherd chuckled. "Now, stay put."

Detective. I loved the sound of that word attached to that name. I'd recently accepted an entry-level job as beat cop with BCPD and, during a vodka-fueled date, sheepishly admitted to Shepherd that my goal was to work my way up to be a detective. Without hesitation, without doubt or humor, Shepherd fully supported and encouraged this.

You can do it, he'd said, chin lifted, truth in those dark eyes.

That day, we were both on a high as Shepherd had received a seventy-five cent an hour raise as assistant project manager at Pro Windows and Doors, a company he'd been with since he was eighteen. Things were good.

I listened to Shepherd's grunt-laced curse words as he unloaded something heavy from the back of the truck. Back and forth he walked, unloading, moving things around. Then, he disappeared for a few minutes. I was beginning to worry, when I heard footsteps, then, "Okay, we're ready, but keep your fold on, Nancy Drew."

"No," I whined as he opened the passenger door.

"Uh-uh, no peeking."

Groaning, I placed my hand in his as he guided me out of the truck.

"Don't forget to lock it," I said.

"No one's out here and besides, if anyone did want to steal something, they're more than welcome to that piece of junk."

I laughed.

As Shepherd led me down a footpath, butterflies awakened in my stomach.

"Be careful." Shepherd squeezed my hand. "It's muddy here."

"Baby, I'm in flip flops."

I almost screamed when Shepherd swooped down and picked me up, cradling me against his chest like a baby. Love blossomed in my chest and my heart started to beat just a little bit faster.

"This is going to be tricky..."

I held on tightly as Shepherd maneuvered around and then into something, almost falling three separate times in the process. By the time he lowered me onto what felt like a picnic table bench I was more than grateful to be out of the air.

"Just a few more minutes."

After a light splash of water, we began to move. A smile spread across my face when I realized we were in his canoe. It was cute that he thought he could conceal the fact that we were floating through water.

I listened as he pulled in the oars, set them in the bottom of the canoe, then shuffled toward me.

"You ready?" he asked.

"I mean, I think so..."

The blindfold was gently removed from my eyes. The first thing that hit me was the glorious sunset right in front of us. Beams of bright orange and fuchsia shot up from the mountains like spears of light. The colors reflected off the dancing water that surrounded us. The second thing that registered was the picnic— an actual picnic basket—sitting at my feet. The third was the smile on my boyfriend's face.

He cupped my face in his hands and leaned in. The setting sun washed his tanned skin in a beautiful golden glow. He looked like a copper statue, I remember thinking. A gorgeous copper Greek god.

"This is beautiful," I exclaimed.

"I love you, Ro."

A knot grabbed my throat. "I love you too, Shepherd."

His eyes filled with tears and was startled by the rare show of emotion. I hadn't ever seen Shepherd cry before.

He took my hands into his. They were cool and clammy.

My stomach began to swirl with a mixture of nerves and excitement.

"Do you remember the first time we met?" he asked, his voice cracking.

Tears filled my own eyes. I nodded, swallowing deeply.

"There's something I didn't tell you."

"What?"

"I kept that pen."

I chuckled. "That's okay. I have more."

"No, Ro, I mean I kept it because I wanted to remember that day for the rest of my life. I knew there was something special about you from the moment I laid eyes on you in that stupid, awful children's shelter. You were like a ray of sunshine in a world of black. What you don't know is that I used that pen— your pen—to finish high school, to sign the paperwork on my first job, to sign the loan on my first car, to write a letter to my father."

"Oh my God, Shep." Tears rolled down my cheeks.

"I used that pen for every monumental thing in my life." He was crying so hard that he used the back of his hands to wipe away his tears. "And now... Now I'd like to use it to apply for a marriage license with you."

I began sobbing.

Shepherd gently grabbed my face, tilting it up to meet his own teary eyes.

"You say that I saved you, but Rowan, you are the only reason I am still alive, too. You are the only reason I get up every morning. You are the only reason I remember how to smile. In this crazy, fucked up world, Rowan, you are my sunshine. Please marry me. Please be my wife. I love you, Rowan.

"I love you.

"I love you.

"I love you."

THIRTY-SEVEN

AMBER

Mark is sitting on the back patio when I get home at half past eight. Unusually late for me, but after receiving Emma's request to meet her, I couldn't say no.

That's a lie. I jumped at the chance to avoid going home. It's been a hell of a day, starting with spending the morning at the clinic getting Connor's bloodwork done for his tests. He screamed bloody murder and had to be held down. It was awful. And just now, over cocktails with Emma, I broke down. Literally, sobbed like a baby right there in the restaurant. I had to spend twenty minutes in the parking lot gathering myself and fixing my makeup before coming home. I want it done, I've decided. When I meet with the divorce attorney next week, I want to draft the paperwork. Rip off the band aid, so to speak. I want out of my marriage.

I pause at the sliding glass door and watch my husband. He is blankly staring into the darkness of our small back yard. Despite the cold and drizzly weather, he is wearing a T-shirt and his feet are bare, kicked up on an overturned trashcan.

I lean against the wall and a feeling of deep sadness comes over me.

How will he react when I tell him I'm leaving him?

How will Connor react to the separation?

How will *I* react to *their* reactions? Will I stay strong or will I crumble under guilt? Will I wimp out and justify "staying for the kids"? Will I remain miserable for the rest of my life? Will I forget that I deserve to find true happiness?

As if sensing me, Mark turns his head. His profile is illuminated by the dim light pooling from the kitchen window.

I open the door and step outside, the chill in the air sending goosebumps over my arms.

"Hey." I wrap my arms around myself. "God, it's cold out here."

"How's Emma?" he asks.

"A mess." *As am I*.

"Where did you guys go?"

"Well, she was at Last Call, but I didn't want to go there, so we met at Dos Tacos."

"What's going on with her?"

"She's thinking about moving, actually. Taking another job."

"Really? Hasn't she only been at the elementary school for a few years now?"

"Three years, yeah."

"Why does she want to leave?"

"To be honest I don't really know what's going on with her. She's thinking about moving back to Houston, where she grew up." *To be honest, dear husband, we really didn't talk about her that much because I was too busy talking about how I am going to leave you.*

"Houston?" he scoffs. "Why would anyone want to move back to that sweltering hellhole?"

"I don't know. She had a fling with some guy but I get the sense something has happened."

"Who?"

"She never told me his name."

"She's so weird."

Yes, she is, and it's what I love most about my best friend. Mark has never liked Emma and has made no effort to conceal his ill feelings—despite having no real reason to dislike her. My opinion? I think Mark doesn't like Emma because he knows, deep inside, that I wish my life was more like hers. Soon, it will be.

"How's Connor?" I ask.

My husband turns away and my mommy instinct surges to life. I haven't seen Connor since I left for work before lunch— over nine hours ago—and I feel guilty about that. That goddamn guilt that plagues me. The guilt I feel for being happy at work, or with Emma, or being by myself, instead of being where I should be—with my child.

"Did something happen?" I ask.

"He threw a fit."

"Okay... he throws lots of fits..."

"No, he really freaked out."

"He spent the morning at a clinic getting blood drawn. It was a hard day for him. What happened?" I glance over my shoulder toward his bedroom.

"He got so frustrated over that stupid video game I was letting him play on his iPad. He threw it on the ground."

"I told you not to let him play that game. He's too young. We're setting a bad precedent. People get real addictions to video games. We've talked about this."

"Well, don't worry. He's grounded from all his devices for twenty-four hours."

"Where is he?"

"In his room. I locked him in there."

"You *locked* him in there?"

"He couldn't control himself, Amber," Mark snaps and I'm taken aback by the outburst of emotion. "The kid has to learn to control himself—the kid has to be disciplined."

"Mark, there's something wrong with him cognitively—"

"Bullshit, Amber. You're basing that off of one person's assessment. And besides, even if there is something wrong with his brain, do you mean to tell me that we're not supposed to discipline our kid?"

I inhale to argue back, but bite my tongue. Mark is never going to understand Connor—or me for that matter—and before too long I'm going to be out of this marriage anyway. Arguing with him is not worth it—not anymore.

Without giving Mark the courtesy of a response, I hurry to Connor's bedroom. My stomach sinks when I see the door shut. We never *ever* fully shut the door to Connor's room.

Quietly, I unlock and push the door open.

The overhead lights are on, along with the two bedside lamps. He must've been scared. Connor is curled into a ball in the middle of the floor. My heart breaks. Slowly, I tiptoe across the room and kneel down, cursing my popping knees as I do so. He doesn't stir.

I swipe a piece of that beautiful brown hair from his forehead.

He's obviously been crying. His eyes are matted and dried snot circles his nose.

Tears fill my eyes. I'm a terrible mom.

I should have been here.

"We'll figure out what's going on with you, baby," I whisper. "Don't worry, Mommy will fix this."

THIRTY-EIGHT

ROWAN

It is eleven o'clock when I hear my husband pull into the garage. I surge out of the armchair where I've been waiting for him since stalking him at Last Call. My heart begins to race. I tiptoe-jog to the bedroom and quickly light all nine candles that I spent thirty minutes strategically placing around the room.

The house door opens.

I dart into the bathroom and check the mirror. The makeup I applied two hours earlier has faded, but still looks decent. Thick eyeliner, dark eyeshadow, and bright red lips to match the lingerie draped over my naked body. I pinch my nipples until they are erect, then fluff my hair to add volume. Luckily, I've had just enough wine to deaden the insecurity that I would normally feel when seeing the fat rolls pooching around the delicate strings of the lingerie. I remind myself that there is only one part of me that my husband is interested in, and that's between my legs.

I run back into the bedroom, grab the bottle of champagne I purchased on the way home, and turn toward the door, ready.

Footsteps down the hall.

My heart is racing, my palms slick against the chilled bottle.

The footsteps take a detour and disappear into the kitchen.

"Dammit," I mutter. *Come on, come on, come on...*

Finally, my husband appears in the doorway.

Despite the nerves coursing through my veins, I smile the calm, confident, seductive smile I practiced in the mirror earlier.

Shepard's jaw unhinges.

This reaction pleases me.

"Welcome home," I say, popping the cork. Careful to angle my body so that he doesn't notice the fat rolls, I pour two glasses of champagne.

Shepherd is frozen in place as I pad across the room and hand him one of the glasses.

"You look—" he stutters, "you look amazing."

"Thank you. I thought we could spend a bit of time together before going to sleep tonight."

"O—okay. Where's Aunt Jenny?"

"She's staying at the facility tonight. It's just us."

"Where's Banjo?"

"Outside."

I take his hand that isn't holding the champagne and guide him to the bed. As I do so, I inhale, searching for her scent on him, but smell nothing but whiskey and cigarettes. After positioning my husband at the edge of the bed, I drop to my knees.

I remove his shoes, his socks, work my way up to his belt, his pants.

He is rock-hard as I pull down his boxer briefs.

I hear him chug the champagne above me.

Wrapping my hand around the shaft of his penis, I take him in my mouth as far as I can. My eyes water, and for a second I'm afraid I might throw up. I think of *her* being there before me, the smell of *her*, the taste of *her*.

Off.

Get off *my husband.*

Shepherd groans as I stroke back and forth. "Jesus baby."

He grabs a chunk of my hair in his fist. Holding me in place, he forces himself down my throat, as he does every time. Tears roll down my cheeks. My skin ignites with adrenaline from the pain and disgust of it. The ardent urge to attack him is so fierce that I have to clench my hands into fists at my side.

When I know he is close, I release him and rise to my feet, forcing poise.

As I take the empty glass of champagne from his hand, I imagine shattering it against the night stand and shoving the broken stem into his jugular. Instead, I shove him onto the bed, and straddle him, pulling aside the red lingerie before lowering onto his shaft. And with the candlelight dancing over our naked bodies, I ride my husband until he bellows my name.

My name.

THIRTY-NINE

AMBER

"I want a divorce."

Mark freezes, mid-bite, the plastic spoon halfway to his mouth. He looks up from his late-night snack. A cup of yogurt—no-sugar, no flavor, just like him.

A moment passes as we stare at each other.

Oh my God, I said it.

I did it.

My heart pounds underneath my nightgown. My mouth is dry. My knees are weak. I have to fight from gripping onto the doorway for support. I'm a mess.

After checking on Connor, I attempted to relax with a bottle of wine and a bath. Instead, I found myself stewing. I couldn't believe Mark locked our son in his room. After emptying the bottle, I gave myself a pep talk in the mirror and, well, here I am.

Choose the right time, I tell my clients who are on the edge of divorce. *Don't tell your spouse you want a divorce the minute before he is supposed to walk out the door to work, or before a visit to the in-laws. But also understand that there is never going to be the perfect time to end your marriage. There will always be future plans, financial uncertainty, an upcoming birthday...*

I realized today what bullshit that advice is. Because, at some point, the spouse who wants the divorce breaks, and everything spills out with zero thought to day or time. Just like me, right now.

Mark's mouth opens, closes... opens, closes. He's completely stunned. Blinking, he drops his spoon in the cup. He closes his eyes and shakes his head. A flush of red races up his neck.

Abruptly, he pushes back from the dinner table, sending his chair tumbling backward as he surges up.

The burst of noise sends my heart jumping into my throat. I glance over my shoulder where Connor is sleeping down the hall.

"I can't believe this." Mark's hands curl into fists, his chest swelling like a bear puffing himself up for a fight. He's furious—and I am dumbstruck. I'm not sure what I expected but it was not this. This is the most emotion I have seen in my husband in ages. Hell, I can't remember the last time he was mad. Really mad.

"Why?" Mark demands. "Why, Amber?"

And in that simple, three-letter word, my resolve weakens. *Why.*

How can I accurately explain *why* when I am so overwhelmed with nerves that I can't even form a thought in my head? I've spent hours, days, months—years—practicing what I would say during this moment. Yet it feels like all the bravery and courage vanished the moment he wants to understand more about it. To talk about it. To make it real. I realize then that I am ill-prepared for this moment. I blame the wine.

"Why?" he barks, becoming emboldened by my sudden attack of amnesia. His chest is rising and falling heavily now, reminding me of the time he got into a bar brawl when we were dating decades ago.

Remain calm. (Another piece of advice I give my clients.)

My brain tells my lungs to take a deep breath but the communication gets lost somewhere in the crippling anxiety coursing through my veins.

"I'm not happy," I say with little strength in my voice. "I haven't been for a long time. You know this."

He releases a groan of frustration and grips the top of his head.

Connor stumbles into the room, hair a mess, jammies in a twist, totally oblivious to the drama around him. Neither of us look at him.

"I can't fucking believe this."

"You can't believe this?" I gawk at him. "Are you serious? I have told you countless times I wasn't happy, that I didn't feel content in our marriage."

"I know but we talked about it. And I thought things got better."

"Better?" A humorless cackle escapes my lips. Now I'm getting mad. "Things got better for a little while, yeah, but then they just go right back to the way they were. That's what happens. We talk, things change for a few months, and then they change right back... And also..." I hesitate, but then force myself to say it. "I'm sick of carrying the weight of paying all the bills."

He says nothing, his ego obliterated by the hit. I, on the other hand, feel relief.

"We've talked about it before," I continue. "I even asked you to get another job, one that contributes more to the household bills and our debt—but you won't. You listen but you never take the next step."

"You said you were okay with it, Amber," he sneers.

"*Once.* And I only said it because I felt terrible for even bringing it up. But *seriously,* Mark? Did you really think I'd be cool with us rolling into retirement with you having not only *not* contributed a penny toward it, but also not helped with paying off the debt you and I *both* created?"

"So you were lying when you said you were okay with it."

"I said that once! One time. A long time ago—and I was just trying to make you feel better. I remember that fight. We were both drunk."

"You know what? That's your problem, Amber. You talk out of both sides of your ass."

"No. I *act,* Mark. That's the difference between you and me. When I realized my therapy business wasn't turning enough of a profit to make sense, I shut it down and went to work for someone else. Do you know that you never once said you were sorry to me? Never once offered a shoulder to cry on? That was hard on me, Mark! I failed. I was depressed for months after that. I felt like a laughing stock. But I did what was best for the family."

"Just like you're doing now?"

"Fuck you. I'm sick of it—all of it. And just like my business, when I knew it wasn't going to work, I made a change. *That's* what I'm doing right now. You and I," I gestured between us, "we don't work. So I'm going to make a change."

"You are..." His jaw clenches. "Unbelievable, do you know that? Selfish—you're selfish. You always have been. I can't believe you're doing this."

Connor is now weaving in and out of the table legs while humming—loudly—a song he must have heard while watching cartoons. He's doing this because he's either picked up on the drama and feels uncomfortable, or he can't read a freaking room —just like his dad.

"What about him?" Mark gestures to Connor under the table.

"I don't know. I haven't thought that far ahead. But we'll figure that out. That's what lawyers are for."

The second the word *lawyer* rolls off my tongue, Mark

snaps. Spinning on his heel, he sends his fist into the kitchen wall, blasting a hole through the sheetrock.

"I can't believe you're doing this! And right now, too! Right when we've got all the stuff going on with Connor. Damn you Amber, you can't even wait for things to calm down, can you?" His face is red, veins bulging from his neck.

In response to his father's outburst, Connor begins singing at the top of his lungs.

I'm in the middle of a fucking madhouse. I want to cover my ears and run away. Damn them both.

"What about my business?" Mark yells. "Are you going to take half of that?"

"No. Of course not! I wouldn't touch your business and am hoping, in return, you won't touch my retirement account."

His jaw drops. "I *cannot* believe this."

Connor has found a crayon and is now coloring on the walls as he sings.

Mark begins fanatically shaking his head. "I can't do this. I can't only see Connor every other week. You can't do this to me —I can't ..."

Tears swim in his eyes despite the rage contorting his face. I cannot believe I'm witnessing this. Mark has taken exactly zero interest in Connor's life, and all of a sudden, he can't imagine being without him for a few days?

"What about the house?" he croaks. "What about all our debt? What about—"

"The lawyers handle all that kind of stuff."

"And who's going to pay them?"

All practical questions, none that I have answers for.

He studies me closely for an excruciating minute. "Is your life really that bad, Amber? Is our life really so bad that you are willing to rip this family apart? Make Connor go between houses every other week, every holiday? Make him become a child of divorce?"

My stomach rolls. I'd figured all this out in my head, told myself that I—we—could do it, yet the moment I am met with adversity my resolve completely evaporates. I doubt everything —every word I've said. Because, truly, my life really isn't that bad. It's just loveless.

Mark rights the chair he knocked over, sinks down, and drops his head in his hands.

"I'll do therapy, with you," he whispers on a shaky breath. "I'll try harder, do better. I'll get a new job. I'll close my business and work for someone else, just like you did. Hell, I'll get two jobs. Maybe I could do that—get a night job. Just... Please— please just don't tear this family apart."

This is where ninety-nine percent of the "divorce conversations" fail. The emotions take over and suddenly everything seems too hard, too painful, too difficult to navigate. And instead of standing our ground, we cave.

This is where I am supposed to *be firm*, as I tell my clients. Here, I am supposed to say: *No therapy, Mark. I want a divorce. My decision is final.*

But I don't.

Instead, I watch Connor crawl to my husband, wrap his arms around Mark's legs, and rest his little head on his thigh.

"Don't cry, Daddy," he says, "don't cry."

Connor looks back at me, his chin quivering.

Tears fill my eyes.

How the hell can I do this? How can *anyone* do this?

How can anyone put their family through this?

FORTY

ROWAN

After pouring a glass of whiskey to ease the pain between my legs, and the disgust in my heart, I head down to the basement, clicking on the floor lamp at the base of the stairs.

Banjo follows seconds later, excited at this midnight activity.

I check my cell phone but don't click into Kellan's messages. I feel guilt for having just had sex with my husband. I feel guilt for only doing it because I couldn't stand the thought of him being with another woman and wanted to remind him that *I am his wife*. More than all that, I feel guilt for hating every second of it.

After a glance over my shoulder, I power up the computer and settle into the orthopedic rolling chair Shepherd insisted on buying. Two thousand dollars, and he gripes about me spending eighty on running shoes?

Banjo dips under the desk and curls into a ball at my feet.

When the browser pops up, I click into the search box and type: *Emma, Allen Elementary, Blackbird Cove*

A picture of Emma's face fills the screen under the headline of "Faculty."

I stare at the woman. A picture of perfection, staring back at me. In my mind's eye, I picture her with my husband, straddling him as I just did. Was she better than me? Probably so.

In under five minutes, I learn that Emma is seven years younger than me, has no criminal record, is not married, and has no kids, though in an interview for the school newspaper she is quoted saying that she "can't wait to have a soccer team of children of her own." Emma appears to be single based on the lack of men in her social media feeds. She likes cats, shopping, Pilates, and mimosa-fueled brunch with her friends. There are several pictures of her and Amber, mostly sharing drinks.

In summary, Emma is my exact opposite.

I zoom in on an image of her arm. Though blurred, I can tell she has multiple tattoos, but can't quite make them out. I can't tell if any of them resemble the tattoo Shepherd recently got.

I scroll through her social media feeds for any link to the symbol of Zhiva, the Slavic goddess, that now graces my husband's wrist.

I take a sip of my wine, stare at the screen, while scratching Banjo's back with my bare toe.

I search for mythology quotes, anything Slavic, anything mystic. I find nothing.

After a few more fruitless searches, I click into history to delete all evidence of my searches, but pause, scanning the history tabs.

I set down my wine and lean in.

After a few link-clicks, the face of another woman fills my screen. Her name is Cora Granger, a former social worker turned stay-at-home wife. Cora has no social media, nor does her husband Jack, who owns the local plumbing company.

I lean back and stare at the image on the screen.

FORTY-ONE

AMBER

I'm drunk. Honestly? Not nearly drunk enough.

After my failed I-want-a-divorce speech, I pried a crying Conner from his father's legs, scooped him into my arms, and carried him to bed. There, I had to read him two bedtime stories to get him to fall asleep again.

He asked why daddy was crying. *Because Daddy doesn't feel good,* I'd said. *Does he need to go have blood taken?* he'd asked. *No,* I'd said.

Then, he asked why I wanted to rip the family apart (using the words he'd heard from Mark). *Our family will always be together,* I'd said.

I'm mad at myself. No, that's not the right word. I'm disappointed in myself. I'm questioning all the times I thought my husband didn't love me. If he truly didn't love me, he would have simply let me go, right? He wouldn't have gotten so angry at the mention of divorce. He wouldn't have offered to do couples' therapy. He wouldn't have offered to "do better." And he certainly wouldn't have offered to get a night job.

How could I have been so unequivocally certain that I

wanted a divorce—for *years*—yet in a short, five-minute argument, question everything?

Maybe Mark really does love me. Maybe there is a chance. Things would certainly be easier if we stayed together. Splitting up the assets and debt, living on my own, sharing custody—all that is hard. The lifetime of guilt that accompanies all of it? That's even harder. Maybe we could make it work. After all, like Mark said, my life really isn't *that* bad.

These thoughts war with the practical side of my brain that is telling me that I have, once again, allowed fear to stop me.

What would I tell my clients right now?

I would remind them that they have a choice, that they are not stuck. By not following through with the divorce (wimping out), they have (indirectly) made a decision. In choosing to stay in their marriage, they must try to do everything they can to make things better or simply accept that this is their life.

I once told a client who wanted to leave her husband, but couldn't pull the trigger, to simply remove the expectations she had of her spouse. This way, she wouldn't be so disappointed by him all the time.

As I sit here now, I think: how horrible is that? What kind of life is that?

I push away the glass of wine and decide that it is all too much right now.

I'll put it all aside, until tomorrow, anyway.

My gaze lands on the mystery notebook that I'd found in my old client couch, sitting on the coffee table in front of me.

I pick it up, thinking about the poor anorexic, pill-addicted woman who it once belonged to. I wonder if she went through a divorce, or if she, like me, wimped out and made the decision to accept a mundane, dull, passionless life?

Probably so, I muse as I flip open the notebook. I choose a random entry, and begin reading...

The watcher was here again. Outside my house. It was the same person I saw outside the window while I was in the gym. Someone is watching me, I'm sure of it now. I am not crazy. Today they were standing on the shore by the lake, staring up at the house, watching me. This time, I grabbed the binoculars—I'd ordered a pair from Amazon the week before—but the moment I raised them to my eyes, the person turned away before I could see their face. But not before I saw the knife in their hand. A freaking knife. They wanted me to see it. They're messing with me. Tormenting me.

I don't know what to do. I can't go to the police. I can't have them inside my home, asking questions. I can't. I feel trapped. Worse, I feel like I can't get out.

I don't know what to do.

We're scheduled to leave for Spain next week, for a month. Maybe the person will stop coming to the house. Give up on whatever it is they're looking for in me. Is it me?

I hope they're gone.

I hope when I return, I never see that person again.

I slowly lower the notebook onto my lap, my mind spinning.

Anorexia.

Xanax.

Spain.

Slowly, a woman's face materializes behind my eyes. Short, brown hair, rail thin, sickly appearance, a large, dark mole above her left eye. I remember the mole specifically, because I wondered why she never had it removed.

I remember—I finally remember. I know who the notebook belongs to.

She was a client of mine for three months. Or was it four?

Her name is Cora Granger.

Cora is a social worker. She came to see me about her anxiety, which I quickly realized had spun into an eating disorder. Cora hated her job. She was grossly overworked and underpaid, as most social workers are. She didn't care about her work, that much was obvious, and I remember thinking: *but so many children are counting on you.*

FORTY-TWO

AMBER

"I don't understand why you won't cover this. The order came directly from my son's pediatrician, who has advised us to do the genetic testing." I pivot at the end of the kitchen and retrace the line I've been pacing for the last forty-two minutes that I've been on the phone with our insurance company. Correction: Thirty-five of the minutes I've been *on hold* listening to staticky music that makes me want to stick a sewing needle through my eye. After receiving a "you may owe" email from Connor's clinic, regarding the testing for which we'd *already* completed the blood work, I called our insurance company.

It's only eight forty-five in the morning.

Connor is at the breakfast nook, poking around at a bowl of Coco Puffs, staring blankly at the morning news I'd turned on while waiting, pacing the floor.

"I understand, ma'am," the agent says, "but genetic testing is not covered for the symptoms your doctor provided."

"Who says? Who decided that it's not covered?"

"The plan that your insurance is under, ma'am. I can send you—"

"No. Is genetic testing covered at all? Anywhere on the

plan? We already submitted the bloodwork." *And yes, I know I should have called beforehand to ensure it was covered.*

"Yes, I believe it is covered under certain circumstances."

Mark walks into the kitchen, showered, ready for a day sitting in his handyman office staring out the window. We haven't spoken since last night, when I'd mentioned the D-word. Unlike him, I haven't slept. After realizing who the note-book belonged to, I retreated to the garage and read Cora Granger's file cover to cover. Later today, I plan to get in touch with her and make sure she's okay.

Mark pours the last of the coffee into an old, stained travel mug with the image of Burt Reynolds's face on the side. I hate that mug. I also wanted that coffee.

I turn away.

"So change the circumstances," I snap, my patience cashed out. "I can call my pediatrician and have her submit a different code to for the testing. What codes cover genetic testing?"

"I can't—I'm not sure—"

"Give me the list of diagnostic codes in which you will cover genetic testing, then I'll give those to my doctor and she'll use one of those. I'll wait while you look them up."

"Uh, ma'am, they're linked under many different diagnoses that may not correspond with—"

I clench my jaw and stifle a scream. "Fine. Just tell me how much it will be out of pocket?"

"How much is what?"

"Genetic. *Testing,*" I seethe.

The sound of the agent's nails clicking the keyboard tap through the phone like ice pelting glass. I want to throw the phone through the window.

"For a full gene panel," she says, "it's $1,200, estimate."

Estimate.

"How much for the whole exome? The one that looks

deeper into the genes? They said we might have to do that next."

"$2,750, estimate."

"Christ." I shake my head. "While I have you, can you confirm that you'll cover his autism testing? It's a full day of testing, I can give you—"

"No, we don't cover that."

I am about to spit every vile word I've ever heard in my life through the phone when a *Breaking News* alert beeps from the television. The banner reads:

Local woman found murdered—third victim in less than a week.

Above the banner is a picture of Cora Granger.

The phone drops from my hand.

FORTY-THREE

ROWAN

"I thought you were going to work today?" Shepherd asks as I walk into the kitchen in a long sleeve T-shirt and sweatpants.

I lower into a seat at the table, across from him. A coffee cup steams next to him, the morning paper in his hands. I asked him, long ago, why he prefers the newspaper over the hundred options of online apps available on his phone. He told me he likes the feeling of the paper between his fingertips.

This morning's headline: *Another woman found dead.*

Though the FBI has virtually shut out everyone since finding the third body, I was able to glean some information from Hoffman, who has kept his ear to the ground at the station. Cora Granger was found dead in her home, by her husband, after he'd gotten home from work. Her injuries were similar to the other women's, although Cora had an X carved over her mouth.

"I'm taking some time off," I say, my eyes locked on his. "I just called in. I'm going to take the week off, at least."

"Time off? You've never taken a week off work." He tilts his head to the side, regarding me closely. "Especially with all this stuff going on," he lifts the paper. The entire front page details the homicides of Alyssa Kaing, Macy Swift, and Cora Granger.

"The feds have taken over those cases," I shrug.

His eyes narrow.

I pick at a speck of dried something stuck to the table. "Also, I've decided that I'm going to move Aunt Jenny to that facility in Dallas, the one I talked to you about a few days go. I'm going to go to the facility this morning to talk to them about it. Anyway, when we go, I thought you could come with me. You and I could spend some time together after she gets settled. You know, get out of town for a bit. Maybe go on a proper date."

He stares at me like I have horns growing out of my head.

"Oh, and I noticed the computer downstairs in the basement is running hot. I'm going to take it to that electronic shop, Java Fix, to check it out. Maybe have the fan replaced."

An alert vibrates from Shepherd's phone. I'm not sure if it's a call or a text, but it takes everything I have not to snatch it and check the sender.

A beat passes as Shepherd and I stare each other, him careful to keep his eyes on mine and off his phone—or perhaps careful to make sure I don't see what's on his phone.

Nerves inch up my back.

"Shepherd." I lean in. "Are you okay?"

"Yeah, why?"

"You'd tell me if something was going on, right? We promised, remember? No secrets. Not between us."

His phone vibrates again.

Our eyes never leave each other's.

FORTY-FOUR

AMBER

Come on, come on... My heart is roaring as I pull onto the side of the road. I can't drive. I can't focus. I can't breathe.

His phone goes to voicemail.

"Shit—*dammit.*"

Hands shaking, I open a new text:

> Me: We need to talk immediately.

I set the phone on my lap—anxiously awaiting his response —and stare at the new tattoo on my wrist. Usually, I keep it concealed by wearing a watch over it, but this morning, I forgot. I rub my thumb against it. *I need you, I need you, I need you...*

When there is no response, I type again.

> Me: Call me. Now. It's extremely important.

No response.

> Me: It's about the woman who was just found.
> CALL ME.

I feel like I'm going to throw up.

Five minutes pass, no response.

He must be with Rowan.

I bang my palms against the steering wheel.

"*Dammit*, Shepherd."

FORTY-FIVE

ROWAN

After speaking with the staff at the assisted living facility about Aunt Jenny's move, I went to her room.

I noticed immediately that she was distant, lost somewhere between the cracks of this horrible, horrible disease.

I pull a chair next to her bed, where she lies on her back, relaxed against stacked pillows. Her hands are folded over her stomach. I notice her bare fourth finger and a deep sadness comes over me. Aunt Jenny's ex-husband and estranged son care so little about her that they are unwilling to come to her aid during the final phase of her life. Jenny will die all alone, no soulmate, life-partner, to hold her hand.

"Good morning, Aunt Jenny," I say gently.

When I receive no response, I settle into the chair and quietly watch the shallow rise and fall of her chest as our last conversation about my marriage trickles through my memory.

"Aunt Jenny, Shepherd said you snapped at him this morning."

"I don't remember."

"Well please try to remember that's it hard for him to have someone else living in the house now."

"It's hard for me to see you with him."

"Jenny, that's not nice."

"He's no good for you, Rowan."

"Why do you say that?"

"He is your everything, but you are not his. It's always been that way. From the first day I met Shepherd, I noticed how you tended to his every need, from refilling his drink to clearing his plate after lunch. All these years later, you still do that, but never once have I seen him do that for you." A moment passed. "It was exactly like this with your mother and father."

I bristled, but fought the defensiveness that shot up my spine the moment she mentioned my parents. The doctor warned us that aggression and mood changes were a common side effect of Alzheimer's. His advice? Ride it out.

"Your mother, my sister, was always so insecure," she continued. "Always dependent on others for her self-worth. She married your dad two days after she turned eighteen, despite our parents' protest. She stayed with him no matter what he did. I remember one time, at two in the morning, she called me, begging for bail to get him out of jail. She was completely inconsolable, completely out of her head with worry for him. She could not live a single day without him. He was her entire purpose for life."

"And I, her child, was not."

"That's correct. And I see her in you, Rowan."

"That's why I'm not having kids, Aunt Jenny."

"No, you aren't hearing me. Your marriage is uneven."

"Shep is looking for a job. He'll get back to work soon."

"I'm not only speaking financially. I'm talking abut emotionally. There is no empathy in that man, whatsoever. It's odd. You bend over backward for him but there is no return in favor."

I looked down, took a deep breath.

"At the end of the day, Rowan, someone has to break the cycle. Someone has to stand up and say, this is not good for me..."

Jenny's eyes open. She turns her head to me, her gaze intense as if she can hear my thoughts.

There is no *well, hello,* or, *good to see you.* Instead:

"What's wrong, Rowan?"

To my complete shock, a flood of emotions rushes through my chest. Tears fill my eyes, a knot grabs my throat.

"Jenny," I say, all but choking on the words. "Things aren't okay."

"I know, Rowan."

"No, you don't. It feels like..."

"What?"

"I feel like things are starting to fall apart. Like my entire world is crumbling around me and I don't know what to do."

"Then stop. Stop and breathe. Don't do anything else."

"It's past that point now."

"What's one of the problems?"

"I think Shepherd is cheating on me."

"Then leave him."

"It's not that simple."

"Yes, it is."

"Things are really, really complicated right now. Jenny, I ..." Sniffing, I angrily swipe a tear from my cheek. "I've made some bad decisions. Really bad decisions."

"Can you fix them?"

"No." I am sobbing so hard I can barely speak. "Not this time."

"Is it bad?"

"Yeah. It's really bad."

"Can you talk to me about it?"

"No."

"Why?"

"It could get you in trouble."

"I'm already in trouble," she grins, referring to the fact she has one foot in the grave.

"Stop it, that's not funny."

"I know, sweetheart. Tell me this, then: Why did you make the bad decisions in the first place?"

I drag my fingers through my hair. "I don't know."

"Yes you do."

FORTY-SIX

AMBER

My heart feels like it's about to explode as I climb the steps to the police station.

A receptionist looks up from behind a pane of bullet-proof glass. She presses a button and leans into the speaker box. "Hi there, how can I help you?"

"Hi," I say, my voice unnecessarily loud and squeaky with adrenaline. "I just called—I think it was you who I spoke—"

"Ah, yes. Mrs. Bailey..." The woman types feverishly into her computer. "May I see your driver's license, please?"

My hand trembles as I open my wallet and produce the card.

I look around the waiting room as she enters my information. The room is empty, thank God.

Finally, "Please have a seat, Mrs. Bailey. I forwarded your concern to our on-call officer. He'll will be with you in just a second."

I don't sit. I can't, I feel like I am about to jump out of my skin.

I check my phone again. Shepherd still hasn't texted back. It both infuriates and worries me. We have a pact to never message each other's personal cell phones, and to only communicate through burner phones, but this was too important. I don't care if our affair comes to light.

Especially not now.

I begin pacing back and forth, wondering how I could have been so stupid. It was right there in front of me the entire time. Right there in the notebook. Three women are dead because of me. *Three* women.

The thought rattles me to my core and a sudden panic grips me. Not for the women—for myself. What will be the consequences of what I am about to do?

I haven't thought this through.

What am I doing?

What am I doing?

I am just about to make a run for it when the door opens and Detective Kellan Palmer steps into the waiting room with a startling sense of urgency on his face. Apparently, they'd bypassed the on-call officer and went straight to a detective. I instantly recognize him from the few times I've seen him around town. For a split second, I am taken aback by how attractive the man is this close up. Though I've never officially met him, I've heard plenty about the former marine. Kellan Palmer is the most eligible and desired bachelor in town. Now I can understand why. As he strides across the waiting room, there is an air of confidence and intimidation about him. Very alpha-hero, very sexy.

"Mrs. Bailey." We shake hands and I'm acutely aware of how clammy mine must feel. "Come in; right this way."

I follow Detective Palmer through a heavy steel door. A row of offices line the left side of the hall; to the right, a large space is divided into a dozen cubicles. I feel as though everyone is staring at me.

We step into an interview room and for a second I worry that I am on the verge of an actual panic attack. I remind myself of what I tell my clients: focus on the now, to what is immediately in front of you, in *this* moment. Sight, smell, taste, touch, sound.

The detective gestures to a blue plastic chair tucked under a white folding table and I sit before my knees give out. He rounds the table and sits facing me.

"Thanks for meeting me," I blurt, my nerves getting the better of me. I can't take this stress another minute.

My words tumble out in one long sentence. "I've got to be honest with you, I feel like I should've called a lawyer. I don't want be associated with any of this. I want to remain anonymous. You have to understand that I didn't know... I promise. I have a son, he's special needs, I can't get in trouble. I have to be here for him, I have to—" The last word is cut off by a sob that explodes out of me. Tears run down my face. I am absolutely humiliated. I'm a therapist, for God's sake. My entire job is to teach people how to control their emotions.

Detective Palmer plucks a handful of tissues from a box sitting in the windowsill and sets them in front of me.

"Just start at the beginning. Take your time. There's no rush," he says, though his words don't match his demeanor. He is stiff as an iron rod, staring at me with a tight, tense expression on his face. If anything, Detective Palmer seems as uptight as I am.

I swallow the knot in my throat. "I recently changed jobs. Well, technically, I kept the same job, but moved to a different clinic."

"You're a therapist, correct? At Oak Tree Counseling?"

"Yes, and before that I owned Bailey Counseling. Anyway, we—my husband and I—are going to sell all the furniture from my old office. While cleaning out the couch, I found a notebook tucked underneath one of the cushions: small, like the size of a paperback. One of my old clients must've accidentally left it behind and it slipped behind the cushions. Anyway, it appeared to be a food diary of sorts—like an accountability tracker people keep when trying to lose weight."

I begin shredding the tissue between my fingertips. "About midway through the notebook, the entries stopped being about food and instead, talked about how the woman thought someone was following her, and watching her from outside her home. She said she was scared. To be clear, I thought at this point that the woman could be delusional, because of all the Xanax and wine references, so I wasn't sure if what she was writing was real."

My voice begins to shake. "Last night, I was reading it again and one of the entries mentioned a trip to Spain. I remembered a client from my old clinic talking about an upcoming vacation to Spain and how nervous she was because she hadn't lost the weight she'd wanted to beforehand—she suffered from body dysmorphic disorder and anorexia. That's when it hit me. The client's name was Cora Granger—the woman who was found murdered last night. It was then that I realized that *all three* of the women who have been murdered recently were clients of mine at one point or another. Alyssa Kaing, Macy Swift, and Cora. *And* all three of these women had either confessed to, or greatly implied, being involved in some sort of child neglect."

"Explain," he says, his expression remaining hard and incredibly intense.

"Alyssa Kaing was battling PTSD from a traumatic experience she had with an ex-boyfriend who abused her and his daughter. Alyssa, who was into drugs at the time, never told anyone that he abused his daughter, and years later, his daughter died from mysterious circumstances. She'd turned a blind eye and felt terrible guilt from it. This is why she sought therapy.

"And Macy Swift, the second woman who was murdered, ran a charity for sick kids. During one of our sessions, she told me that she thought her husband was stealing from the charity. I didn't believe her, instead, I believed *she* was stealing from her own charity because after every fundraiser she had, she'd walk in with a new shiny handbag and brag about how she'd gotten an influx of cash. I couldn't stand the woman.

"And then, Cora Granger—she was a social worker. She hated her job and admitted to me that with several cases, she'd sign off on an investigation without due diligence. She would constantly gripe to me about the paperwork and red tape involved in the process. In one case, the child ended up in ICU the next month—a terrible thing that, honestly, was her fault for not investigating properly."

My heart is beating so hard that it almost hurts. Tears well up again, and there is nothing I can do to stop them. "If it's true the women were killed for what I just told you, there is only *one* person I told these details to. Only *one*. And that person is Detective Rowan Velky."

Detective Palmer stares at me, the tension in the room so thick it feels suffocating.

"I bet there's a record of it somewhere," I say. "I'm sure Detective Velky took some sort of notes on what I told her."

"There's nothing. Nothing on record to connect all three women."

I blink. "Really? But the reason I told her was so that she could investigate the families of the women. That's what—"

"Tell me everything about how and when you told her."

"Well, I'd become concerned about what these clients had confided to me, but there wasn't enough evidence to file an official complaint against them—and you know, client/patient confidentiality is very important in my line of work. But it still bothered me enough that I felt like it was my civic duty to report what I was hearing. They all involved children, and, as a mother, it just broke my heart. It ate at me for months while these women were my clients. So, one day, I invited Rowan— she was court-ordered to see me after an officer-involved shooting, as you know—out for coffee and I told her about the women. I told her I was giving her a heads up, and that perhaps she should look into the families, or call CPS, or do whatever a police officer is supposed to do with a tip. I reiterated to her that I didn't have evidence of child abuse but I just wanted to get it off my chest. I felt like it was my civic duty to do so, you know?"

I scrub my hand over my forehead. "I regretted it the next morning—for so many reasons. One, my clients need to trust me; two, I could lose my job if it got out that I spilled client secrets; and three, I wasn't certain about the accusations I was making in the first place. Anyway, that's the story. That's the whole story... and I felt like you should know."

"So you think Detective Velky killed these three women?"

"I—well, I heard the gossip that they were killed by some vigilante killer who knew their dirty secrets. She's the only person I told their dirty secrets to. She's the only person who knew."

"You also knew their secrets, Mrs. Bailey."

I had expected this accusation, and after a quick inhale, recited the response I'd practiced in the car on the way over.

"True, but I'm sure I have an alibi, as I'm home every night with my husband and son, and work during the day."

Detective Palmer turns his back, walks to the window, and stares into the parking lot. What feels like an eternity passes in silence. I get the feeling that I'm missing something, that there's a lot more to the story than I realize.

That maybe Detective Palmer knew all along.

FORTY-SEVEN
ROWAN

My phone vibrates on the nightstand. Ignoring it, I continue packing clothes into the suitcase I've laid on the bed.

The text is from Kellan, I don't need to check. This makes his twenty-seventh attempt to contact me. Twenty-seven unanswered calls and unopened texts after I told him that I needed a break and asked him to leave me alone. I have too much to deal with right now. In addition to the calls and texts, Kellan has driven by my house multiple times. One time, he even had the balls to pull into the driveway, park, and turn off the engine. There, he sat, his tall, thick silhouette staring into the front window of my home, while my cell phone rang.

Shepherd asked who it was. I told him I didn't know and drew the curtains.

Honestly, it's a bit disconcerting. I don't know what's so important or why he won't respect my need for space. Regardless, I can't deal with it. Not right now.

I'm reaching for the cup of coffee on the nightstand when Shepherd walks into the bedroom. My body tenses.

He joins me at the edge of the bed and scratches Banjo's ears, who is curled next to the suitcase.

"What time are we leaving for Dallas?" he asks.

"Around ten tomorrow. Our appointment with the nursing home is at two in the afternoon. The drive is three hours. I figure we can stop midway and eat lunch. I've already packed up Jenny's things. Oh, and I found a hotel that accepts dogs, so we're good with Banjo."

Shepherd slowly runs his fingers through my hair. Tingles, like fire ants, swell over my skin.

"Are you sure you want to do this, Ro?"

"Yes. Aunt Jenny deserves better care than what I can offer her here."

"Okay." Shepherd looks around the room. "Where is my suitcase? I guess I need to pack some stuff."

"It's in the garage."

As my husband leaves the room, my cell phone lights up again. This time I grab it, turn it off, and hurl it across the room.

FORTY-EIGHT

ROWAN

I awaken on Monday to the sound of crying.

I check the clock, blinking though the heavy haze of sleep. Unable to shut off my brain, I was up all night. The last time I looked at the clock was four-thirty. I must've fallen asleep shortly after.

I look over my shoulder at the indentation of Shepherd's body. The covers are thrown to the side, his pillow askew. He didn't sleep well either.

Frowning, I flip off the covers, slip on my house shoes. Hurrying down the hallway, I pull on my robe, wrapping it tightly at the waist.

Shepherd is sitting at the kitchen table, head in hands, sobbing. On the floor next to him is a shattered cup centered in a puddle of coffee.

My adrenaline surges. Something is very, very wrong.

"Shep!" I rush into the room. "What's wrong?"

"Rowan. I..."

"Talk to me, Shepherd, please."

"I've—I've made some bad decisions," he says.

"I know, I know." I drop to my knees next to him, cutting

my skin on a shard of broken porcelain. I grip onto his thighs, look up at him. "I know, Shep, I know everything. It's okay, I'll fix it. I'll fix all of it."

He frowns, looks down at me. His eyes are so red from crying they look demonic.

Has he taken his pills? Dammit, I should have—

"Fix it?" he asks. "How?"

"Just don't worry. I've got it under control. Just know that I forgive you. I forgive you, I forgive you. We'll fix this."

It has been a very long time since I have seen my husband this emotional.

He drags in a deep inhale, his lip quivering. The tears start again.

"It's just that I've felt so distant from you," he says, wiping his eyes with the back of his hands. "And she, well, she was there."

The instant dropping of my stomach is so intense I feel I'm falling from the sky. My entire body freezes.

I don't speak. I can't.

"I love her, Rowan. I really do."

I release his legs as if they're on fire. Emma's face flashes behind my eyes. So beautiful and perfect.

I scramble backward on my bottom, sliding on the spilled coffee, then push off the floor and stare down at him.

"What?" I say, barely audible. "I thought you were talking about—"

He cuts me off. "I don't want to leave town with you right now, Rowan—I want to leave *you*."

My ears start ringing.

"You want a divorce?"

"Yes."

I grab onto the kitchen counter for support.

"Today, I plan to go visit a lawyer and then she and I are going meet up and figure everything out."

"Emma..." Her name falls from my breathless lips.

Shepherd frowns, stares at me for a minute.

"No, not Emma. Amber. It's Amber."

I don't remember the next few seconds. Only the sound of cars pulling into the driveway, the blue and red lights flashing around the kitchen walls, and Shepherd's voice:

"Rowan? Why are the cops here?"

FORTY-NINE

ROWAN

I whirl around as two unmarked vehicles pull into the driveway, blocking me in. Behind them, a gunmetal-gray Dually rolls up to the curb. Sprinkles of rain begin to fall from the dark, ominous sky above.

I watch two FBI agents get out of the cars, their navy windbreakers flapping against the cold wind. I recognize them as Agents Brian Briggs and Jacob Zeal, the agents who took over the Kaing, Swift, and Granger cases.

"Rowan, what's going on?"

Shepherd rushes by my side. I turn and look at him, wide-eyed, but no words come out.

Boom, boom, boom.

"Shit, get the door, Rowan. What the hell is...?"

The agents stride into the kitchen. The door must have been unlocked.

I say nothing as my wrists are pulled behind my back and secured in handcuffs.

I say nothing as I am dragged outside.

"Rowan Velky, you are under arrest for the murders of Alyssa

Kaing, Macy Swift, and Cora Granger. You have the right to remain silent... "

My eyes lock on Kellan as he climbs out of his truck. The look on his face makes my heart leap into my throat.

Shepherd rushes out the door behind me as another car pulls to the curb, this one with Chief Hood behind the wheel.

"What's going on here?" Shepherd's voice bellows through the quickly rising noise.

Another car.

A rush of strangers.

A woman holding a microphone.

A man, a camera.

"Detective Velky, is it true...?"

Cameras flash in my face...

Kellan's voice somewhere in the mix...

Chaos.

My entire world begins to spin.

Just then a flash of black zips past my peripheral. Banjo leaps to attack one of the journalists.

"No!" I lunge forward, but because my hands are secured behind my back, I have no balance, so I throw my body toward Banjo, attempting to form a barrier between him and the photographer. A body slams into mine. I am twisted mid-air and land on Kellan's body as we hit the concrete with a hard thud.

Banjo whines and nips the air as Shepherd drags him into the garage.

"Are you okay?" Kellan asks, trying to cradle me into his arms, but instead, I am pulled up by an agent and hurried to one of the unmarked cars. The door opens, a hand grips the top of my head and pushes me inside.

The door slams shut.

Faces swarm the windows. Behind them, the agents are trying to clear the crowd. Shepherd is yelling somewhere in the distance.

Noise, so much noise.

The passenger-side door opens and Kellan slips in, quietly closing the door behind him.

"Are you okay?" he hisses, chest heaving. A trail of blood drips down the side of his face from where he hit his head on the concrete after catching me mid-air.

I can't speak. A million words on the tip of my tongue, but none come out.

"Jesus, Rowan," he seethes. "What the hell? I've been trying to call you—to warn you. Rowan, *shit.*" His eyes fill with emotion. "You are in some serious shit, Rowan."

Tears fill my eyes. Over his shoulder I see a journalist trying to get a clear shot of him.

"They're taking your picture, Kellan," I hiss, my voice sounding so small, and disconnected from my body. "They're literally filming you right now. Get out of here. Get *out,* K—"

"Talk to me," he snaps. "Fucking talk to me, Rowan. I'll fix this—just tell me what happened."

"Kellan, leave—"

"Rowan you have to talk to me. I need to understand so I can help. Your therapist, Amber Bailey, told us that she told you about the women." He's speaking so fast my head is spinning. "And they've got a statement from Amos Hoyt who saw you in a baseball cap dumping what appeared to be ashes into the lake next to Mirror Lakes neighborhood the morning after Macy Swift was found dead."

"None of that is enough to convict me, you know that."

"No it's not, but this is: they compared your DNA—which was already in the system—to unnamed DNA found at Cora Granger's murder scene. The captain rushed it through—the DNA matches yours, Rowan. They literally got the results twenty minutes ago, which is why they're here, arresting you. How the hell can you explain that? *Rowan!*" he yells when I don't answer. "How can you explain that?"

The door opens. "What the hell are you doing, son?" Agent Brian Briggs grabs Kellan's arm. "Get out of here."

My heart roars as Kellan is dragged out of the car.

The door slams shut.

Shepherd is surrounded by agents, questioning him. I read his lips: *No, officer, I didn't know a thing. I don't know how she could have done this.*

Our eyes meet.

A single tear runs down my cheek.

FIFTY

AMBER

"Mrs. Bailey, thanks for coming in this afternoon."

"Of course," I say. Although in all honesty, being at this appointment is the absolute last place I want to be right now. Rumors of Rowan's arrest have spread like wildfire. I have two voicemails on my phone from Detective Palmer, and I just missed a call from an agent named Brian Briggs with the FBI requesting to meet with me "asap." Somehow my name was leaked with her arrest and my neighbor just texted me that a journalist is parked outside our home. I had to tell Mark about everything—about the notebook and about my visit to the police station. I wasn't going to but I have a feeling that things are about to spin out of control. To my shock, Mark was mildly empathetic (he's "trying"). He even insisted on coming with me to this appointment, something he would have never done before. But, ironically, I'd rather be here alone. Mark's presence adds a level of stress to my life, and I don't need any extra right now.

I'm sitting here wondering if everyone in this clinic knows that I'm involved in Rowan's arrest, instead of worrying about what the doctor is about to tell us.

The geneticist who ordered Connor's genetic testing lowers himself onto a stool. Two medical students stand behind him; one, a boy, not much more than twenty-one years old with a neck full of acne, and a young woman, maybe five years older, with brown hair and big doe eyes. My gaze flickers to Mark and I wonder what he thinks of the girl. Such an inappropriate thought in the moment.

Connor is kneeling in front of a small chalkboard in the corner of the office, meant to keep kids busy while the doctors deliver test results.

The doctor scratches his chin which is covered in a thick, gray beard. "The good news is that we have found the cause of your son's developmental delays and cognitive impairment."

The *good* news.

"Connor has a rare genetic mutation of unknown clinical significance—this simply means a DNA change that is not fully understood."

Uh. *What?*

He hands Mark and me a stack of papers, each held together by a massive paper clip.

The top reads *Genetic Testing Report*. A dozen words jump off the page at me: *Gene, Mode of Inheritance, Variant, Coding, Zygosity, Classification.* Numbers and letters—so many random letters. I don't understand a single thing. It might as well be in Arabic.

The doctor rolls his chair closer to us and points at the paper. He smells like Old Spice.

"This is the specific gene that is mutated, and this is the spelling change. You can see here, where there is supposed to be a "T", there is a "C.""

I pretend to understand as he goes on to explain the rest of the columns. All I'm thinking is: what does this mean?

"There are only seven known mutations like this in the world," he says. "I spoke with a colleague in Texas who treated a patient with the same mutation, and have been in contact with a few other doctors with similar patients as well. Basically, what we have ascertained with the small pool that we've got to work with is that children with this mutation seem to have developmental delays and cognitive impairment that affect their daily lives, especially in school."

No shit.

"Where did he get it?" Mark asks. (I'm almost as jarred by the fact that he spoke as I am of these bogus test results.)

"Some mutations can be passed down genetically, but considering neither of you seem to have the issues that Connor does, I think it's safe to assume this is not the cause. In this case, it's called *de novo*—you can see that right here on the test results. If not passed down from parents, genetic mutations are, quite frankly, freak accidents of nature."

"They happen the moment the sperm meets the egg," the young woman pipes up from the back.

I have a strong urge to slap her across the face.

"Does it go away?" Mark asks.

"At this current time, there is no cure for genetic mutations —that's the bad news. But my colleague said his patient showed drastic improvement in symptoms with prolonged therapy."

"Hang on," I hold up my hand. "So Conner will have to deal with this for life?"

"Most likely. Yes, ma'am."

My jaw drops. My gaze shifts to my son, who is drawing random shapes on the chalk board, completely oblivious to the life-altering conversation around him.

"Are there any medications for it?"

"Not for genetic mutations, no. But there is a supplement mix that has shown to be beneficial for children with these kinds of issues. I've included it in the paperwork I just gave you. In terms of support there are a few Facebook groups..."

The world around me slows down as I stare at my boy—the creation of a freak accident.

My stomach swirls and for a moment I feel like I'm going to throw up.

Everything is spinning out of control, and I feel powerless to stop it.

FIFTY-ONE

ROWAN

From: PalmerK1982@jjmail.com
To: BanjoForever_RV@jjmail.com
Subject:

Dear Rowan,

They won't let me stay at the station all day and night. Hood forced me to go home and sleep, which I didn't. I can't sleep knowing you're behind bars.

This thing has turned into a shit-show. It's a freaking circus. The media is everywhere. The town is in an uproar. You should know that there are plenty of people who think you are innocent, as do I.

Here's what I know so far. Shepherd has turned over everything to the FBI—cell phones, phone records, iPads, devices, etc. He's given them full access to your home. I haven't spoken to him personally, but I know that he's been in hours of interviews with the feds. He says he didn't know a thing. As far as I know, he is not considered an accomplice.

They had to assign a security detail at Amber Bailey's home. She's getting hounded by the press. She's supposed to meet with the feds this afternoon at two o'clock for her second round of witness interviews. In the first, she told them what she told me. They've requested her clinical files on the three women, as well as your file.

As for me, I've been shut out of the case, because I was your partner and therefore am considered biased. Regardless, I'm keeping my ear to the ground and will update you every second I can. Hoffman has promised me that he'll sneak in his phone to you, every opportunity he can, so we can email back and forth— like this.

Rowan, I want you to be strong. To fight with me. I am here, Rowan, every second thinking of you and actively working to help you. You are not alone. Don't lose hope. I won't.

You are still the greatest woman I've ever met. Do not give up Rowan. I will fight for you.

I will fight for us.

FIFTY-TWO
AUNT JENNY

"I'd like to speak to the judge please."

"Um, ma'am, you're at the police station." The receptionist glances over my shoulder to April, my nurse who I talked into taking me here as driving is no longer an option due to my advancing disease.

"The judge usually works at the courthouse," the receptionist clarifies.

I smooth my dress shirt and lift my chin. I can feel April withering in embarrassment next to me.

"Then I want to speak to someone who's dealing with the Rowan Velky case."

This gets the receptionist's attention. "And your name?"

"My name is Jennifer Willmont. Rowan is my niece."

"Oh, okay. Well, her case is being handled at the federal level. I can call one of the agents who is handling it, but I can't guarantee he'll agree to see you."

"I'll wait."

. . .

An hour later, the heavy steel door opens and a tall, lanky man in a navy suit walks out.

I stand. He offers his hand.

"Ms. Willmont, my name is Brian Briggs. I'm an agent with the FBI. Pleasure to meet you."

"Pleasure to meet you. This is one of my nurses, April. I have Alzheimer's."

"I'm sorry to hear that."

They shake hands.

"I've come to plead for my niece's release," I say.

His brows arch.

"Is there somewhere we can speak in private?"

"Sure."

I ask April to wait outside, then I am led through a large room filled with cubicles. It looks just like you see in the cop shows.

"Please wait here just a second," the agent says. "The room I wanted is currently being used."

I wait as Agent Briggs pulls aside a woman, and quietly speaks into her ear. The woman's gaze sweeps me from head to toe, then she nods and walks away.

"Would you like some water?" he asks as he returns. "Coffee?"

"I'll take a coffee."

I'm taken to a conference room with a long, shiny wooden table and a dozen chairs. There are three people hovered over stacks of papers and photographs. They look up when I enter. I smile, nod.

They frown, look at Agent Briggs.

He says, "Can I get a few minutes in here, please? And can you ask someone to bring in two cups of coffee."

Briggs gestures to the head of the table, the only section that isn't covered with paper. "Have a seat."

"I'd like to be recorded," I say settling into the cold, wooden chair.

Brigg's brow cocks. "No problem. May I ask why?"

"I'm not sure how much longer I'm going to be here and I want my statement to be available for access after I pass."

"I understand. Yes, I'll record this."

"Thank you."

The coffee is delivered along with a small, black recorder. It's placed in the center of the table, between me and Briggs.

I wait until the door closes.

"How is she?" I ask.

The agent hesitates. "Your niece is being taken care of. She's been sectioned off from the other inmates to ensure her safety."

"Good. I wouldn't imagine anyone who served in law enforcement does well in jail, living beside the very people they locked up."

"I can assure you, we are taking all precautions necessary."

I sniff. "Agent Brent—"

"Briggs."

"Briggs, yes. Are you aware of Rowan's childhood?"

"I understand she was placed in foster care at a young age."

"Do you understand why?"

"Her parents were drug addicts, yes."

"There's much more to it than that, sir."

"Indulge me."

I fold my hands in my lap. "When I became Rowan's legal guardian, I noticed almost immediately that she was scared of everything. I mean *everything*. Dogs, cats, frogs, loud noises, crowds, trucks, storms, knocks on the door, even the dark, despite that she was a teenager. She'd jump at everything. It unnerved me, just being around her. Eventually, I allowed her to sleep with me, and that kid would clench onto my arm and never let go, not once, all night long. It was the only way she could sleep."

"That's sad."

"Yes, it was. It took me a long while to realize this was a side effect of being raised in such a dysfunctional family. At the most basic level, Rowan was abandoned from birth, really. She was hardly tended to, dirty diapers all day, and allowed to cry until she vomited. My sister—her mom—took "cry it out" to an abusive level. Rowan was never taught how to regulate emotions. Then they eventually started physically abandoning her at school by not picking her up. Fear of abandonment became as engrained in her psyche as breathing and eating. It became an automatic response. Fear is part of her life, plain and simple."

"I'm not sure I'm following, Ms. Willmont."

"Call me Jenny."

"Jenny, yes, ma'am."

"Because of this, Rowan latches onto anything that provides her a sense of safety—even a false sense. Her husband, Shepherd, gave that to her and she latched onto him with bloody fingernails and never let go. He became her entire world. You see, Rowan is fiercely loyal to those who have helped her—to me and Shepherd. She feels indebted to us."

I raise my hands from my lap and wrap them around the Styrofoam cup, sloshing coffee onto the table.

"I truly believe that if there was a threat to either me or Shepherd, Rowan would kill for us. I think that's true for a lot of families actually."

Agent Briggs dabs up the coffee with a napkin.

A moment of silence spreads between us.

"Thank you for that background information." He clears his throat. "It helps give me a clearer picture."

"She's a good person with good intentions. I want her released from prison."

"I can't do that."

"Yes you can.

"Ms. Willmont, I understand this must be very hard for you, being her family and all. But we have your niece's DNA at Cora Granger's crime scene, and also a clear motive for all three of the homicides." He pauses. "You speak of Rowan feeling indebted to both you and her husband. I understand. But I believe she felt indebted to the community who has supported her, and therefore took it upon herself to rid them of what she considered harmful people."

"I think you're wrong, Agent Briggs."

"I wish I were. Believe me."

FIFTY-THREE

ROWAN

Four months later

I know, from experience, that there is a pivotal point in trauma where the body simply shuts down. The parts of the brain responsible for dealing with emotion become so taxed that they shut off to preserve the parts necessary for survival. Your emotions vanish and your reactions dull, leaving you a shell of a human. A robot. A nothing.

That's how I feel as I stand in front of the judge. Completely void of expression, of feeling life. I'm not hot, I'm not cold, I'm not nauseous, dizzy, or sick.

I'm a dead woman standing.

"All rise," the clerk says. "The honorable Marcus Fitch presiding."

I begin shaking uncontrollably as the judge walks into the room and takes a seat behind the bench.

"Everyone, please take your seat," he says to the room.

Chairs squeak along the tiled floor, followed by a rush of movement as the crowd settles in to witness my fate.

"People of the State of Texas vs. Rowan Velky." The clerk nods to the defense to begin.

"I am Sheri Hobbs," she says, "appearing as counsel for the accused."

"Is this the accused?" the judge asks, gesturing to me.

"Yes."

"How do you plead, Mrs. Velky?"

Tears well in my eyes and I suddenly feel as if I'm suffocating.

"Guilty."

"Mrs. Velky, do you understand the crimes and consequences for what you have just pleaded guilty to?"

"Yes." A tear rolls down my cheek.

"Good. As you both know, the request for a plea bargain was rejected. That said, is there any comment from the prosecution?"

"No."

"Alright then. In the case of the State of Texas versus Rowan Velky, the accused is found:

Guilty of the charge of capital murder for the death of Alyssa Kaing, charged as first-degree murder, and sentenced to life in prison.

Guilty of the charge of capital murder for the death of Macy Swift, charged as first-degree murder, and sentenced to life in prison.

Guilty of the charge of capital murder for the death of Cora Granger, charged as first-degree murder, and sentenced to life in prison.

And finally, guilty of obstruction of justice and seven counts of tampering with evidence, a third-degree felony, in which the accused will pay a $10,000 fine per count..."

His words become muffled, the noise around me suddenly sounding like I'm hearing them while underwater. I grip onto the table, feeling like I'm about to pass out. Closing my eyes, I focus on the sound of the blood rushing through my ears.

Then—

"Request for probation is denied. Is there anything else?"

"No," the prosecutor says.

"Great. Call the next case."

And just like that, it's done.

My life is over.

FIFTY-FOUR

AMBER

Present day

It is a beautiful day. The kind made for long walks, aimless drives, or napping in a hammock under a tree. Spring has always been my favorite season. It's a time of rebirth and renewal, a reset from the darkness and loneliness of winter.

There is no lonely for me anymore. The days, months, years, of longing for someone who understands and appreciates me, who truly loves me, are long gone. I've never been this happy in my life. I now understand everything—the years of angst, the feeling of not being where I was supposed to be, of being trapped in a boring, bleak marriage, and, worst of all, wondering where it all went wrong. All that has prepared for this.

This man. The man who found me at the bar, so long ago, and offered an ear to listen when I felt like no one cared. The man who made me feel wanted, needed, and loved. The man who told me, "Stick with me. I'll take care of you."

Shepherd slips his hand into mine as we step onto the

cobblestone sidewalk that curves through the manicured bushes that line the front yard. The bright morning sun shimmers off a FOR SALE sign next to the front stoop of the home. I look up at him, reveling in that warm feeling he gives me. With just a smile, the man makes my heart skip a beat.

The realtor, Lisa, smiles at my smile, and glances down at my stomach.

"How far along are you two?"

Shepherd beams. "Five months." He gently places his hand on my growing belly. I swear I'm going to have a permanent imprint of his palm above my belly button.

"How wonderful." The realtor glows. "This home is perfect for growing families. Do you have any pets?"

Shepherd and I exchange glances, our smiles wavering.

"Not anymore," he says.

"Oh. I'm sorry." Lisa's expression saddens.

"No, no, it wasn't like that. His name was Banjo, but we gave him up for adoption a long time ago."

"Oh. Well. Hopefully he's in a better place, then. If you choose to get a new dog, the back yard is fenced in and perfect for pets." Lisa looks at Connor who is stuck like glue to my hip. "Are you excited to be a big brother?"

"Yes," he responds politely.

Shepherd reaches around me, rustles Connor's hair, and winks. He is so good with Connor. He is going to be a wonderful father. I know this because he wants to be; he tells me this almost daily. After wanting children for so many years, and Rowan cruelly denying him, Shepherd is consumed by my pregnancy. From the moment our affair began, he expressed his desire to have children with me—with *me*. I'd remind him that he had a wife to consider, but he didn't care. We stopped using protection the moment Rowan was convicted. That exact day, in fact.

I secretly recorded the moment I told Shepherd I was pregnant.

I'd hidden the cell phone behind the toothbrush holder in the bathroom. We were staying at a local hotel, my temporary home after walking out on Mark. It was early, six in the morning, and I'd told him the hot water in the shower wasn't working. When he came into the bathroom, I faced him, naked, beaming from ear to ear, a tissue in one hand and a positive pregnancy test in the other.

He'd cried—actually cried. It was the first and only time I've ever seen Shepherd cry. Then, he dropped to one knee and asked me to marry him. I will never, ever forget that moment for the rest of my life. The next day, Rowan was served divorce papers in prison.

Almost daily, Shepherd tells me he's finally where he's supposed to be. This brings me more joy than I can express. After all he's been through, he deserves to feel happy.

"Also," Lisa adds, her bright expression faltering. "The fence is chain link, but I think I could get the buyer to throw in a discount so that you can replace it with a privacy fence. You can go eight feet tall in this area which would make it virtually impossible to catch a shot of you with a camera."

Shepherd and I share a glance.

The media surrounding Rowan's arrest and eventual conviction was extreme. The story of the haunted small-town detective turned serial killer became sensationalized, dominating both local and national headlines. Our tiny town became a media circus, with journalists from CNN, Fox News, and NBC flying in from all over the country to cover the story. Everyone knows about it. Shepherd and I kept our affair a secret for the first few months after her conviction, until he decided that he was ready to step out publicly. I've always been ready. Since the moment we kissed—an event we celebrated by getting matching tattoos on our wrists—I knew Shepherd was the one for me. I did everything I could in my therapy sessions with Rowan to guide her to leave him. But the woman was loyal, I have to give her that—and also, apparently, the queen of deception. Never, in a million years, did I think Rowan would kill those women. I was as shocked as Shepherd.

Connor kneels down to pick a flower, ignoring the adult conversation above him.

Lisa shakes her head, her face full of sympathy. Although I know it's only for show. "I can't imagine how hard this has been for you guys." Her gaze shifts to Shepherd. "I just couldn't believe it. Literally, I almost didn't believe it. I've met Rowan several times, and I just, wow."

"Well, our focus now is putting one step in front of the other," I say, taking back control of the situation.

It hasn't been easy, the mental and emotional toll it's taken on both of us. Shepherd and I have spent many nights holding each other, sometimes saying nothing, sometimes talking until the sun came up. I've never been more thankful for my background in therapy. All these months later, Shepherd is still unpacking the trauma from being unknowingly married to a serial killer. I can't imagine the effect that would have on someone's psyche. The betrayal alone would be debilitating. Thank God Shepherd has no other mental or health issues to worry about.

I've also filed for divorce. Custody has been easy, as Mark wants to make things as smooth as possible for Connor. When he heard I was pregnant, he actually sent me a text to congratulate me.

It's funny how things work out, isn't it?

I wonder when Rowan will find out about the baby and our engagement.

It doesn't really matter though. She will spend the rest of her life in prison, slowly fading from memory. The town, the media, the world is already beginning to forget her.

Now, it will just be Shepherd, Connor, our yet-to-be-named baby boy, and me. Forever.

The new Velkys.

I can finally see the light at the end of the tunnel.

And I agree with Shepherd. I, too, am finally exactly where I am supposed to be.

FIFTY-FIVE

AMBER

"I'll just have a water," I tell the waiter, patting my belly. I don't know why I feel the need to justify ordering water in a bar; it's obvious I'm pregnant. Regardless, I do every time.

Emma slides her margarita on a coaster and greets me, although I'm not sure how I respond because I am hypnotically staring at the salty condensation dripping from her beveled glass. God, I miss booze. Shepherd won't allow me to take even a sip of alcohol. He's weird about stuff like that—alcohol, drugs. He says he wants a clean lifestyle, for us, and the boys.

"You're glowing," she says.

"Fuck you."

Emma laughs. We both know it's bullshit. Why do people always tell pregnant women such lies?

"Okay, for real, how are you feeling?"

"Like a whale," I groan and rub my stomach again.

Emma wrinkles her nose in sympathy, although I know it's just for show. Only women who have been pregnant truly understand the plights of pregnancy.

"I'm getting heartburn now."

"Oh no. Can you take anything?"

"Shepherd won't let me."

Emma frowns. "What do you mean he won't *let* you?"

I shift in my seat. "He just wants everything as natural as possible."

"Hang on," Emma raises her palms. "Don't tell me he wants you to do a natural birth, too?"

I nod and feel a rush of protectiveness for my soon-to-be-husband. Who is she to judge him?

Quickly, I say, "It's best for the baby, and we want to do everything we can to give this one the best life possible."

Emma stares at me for moment, and for the first time, I can't read her expression. Then, she asks, "How's Connor doing?"

"Good." I shrug. "I think the in-school therapy is helping him."

"Good." She inhales to continue, but then thinks better of it, and closes her mouth.

I'm glad.

Honestly? Ever since Shepherd and I came out publicly, Emma has been, well, different with me. She judges me, as everyone does, for being another man's mistress. I can't really blame her. Emma doesn't understand what it's like to finally meet your soulmate, get pregnant, get engaged. Lately, it feels like she and I live on two separate planets.

"So," she says, twirling the straw in her glass. "How is Shepherd liking his new job as... what was it again?"

"He's a construction project manager, and yes, he loves it. He enjoys it much more than working at the window company he used to work for. Do you know they made him do door-to-door sales for a while? Can you imagine?"

"I didn't know that. Well, that's good to hear. You and Shepherd looked at a house today, right? How was it?"

"We love it. The kitchen needs updating but other than that, it's perfect. I think Shep is going to make an offer tomorrow, using the rest of his severance pay from his old job. I hope the offer goes through because all this house hunting is exhausting me and the baby."

"I bet... Well, thank you for meeting me anyway."

"Of course. It's your last night in Blackbird Cove. You excited to move back to Houston?"

Emma shrugs. "I think so. I'm definitely excited about the pay increase I'm getting by moving to a private school, but I'll miss you, and here. I like it here."

"We'll have a guest room with your name on it."

"Ah, thanks." She glances at her watch, and I realize then that she seems a bit rushed.

"Are you meeting someone else tonight for a proper goodbye?"

She grins. "Yes."

"You know you've never even told me the guy's name. Who have you been secretly running around with?"

"I know, I know..." She looks down and it annoys me.

"Tell me. I'm pregnant and can't get drunk, so I deserve gossip."

"Fine. His name is Chris."

"Does Chris have a last name?"

"Hoffman."

"Sounds like a serious guy. What does he do?"

"He's a cop."

"No way."

"Yep. He works at BCPD."

I still for a moment. "Did he work with Rowan?"

She nods.

"Huh. Ironic."

"Yeah, I know. Anyway. We're super different."

"No kidding—a cop and a free-spirit."

"Right? We've kind of been on and off, but whatever, I'm leaving, so it's done."

"Maybe you two can see each other when you come back to visit me and the baby."

"Maybe." Emma takes a long sip of her margarita. "So... um..."

"What?"

"I have news."

"What?"

"Rowan knows."

"*What?*"

Emma nods, takes another deep sip in a way that suggests she's relieved to have told me.

"How?" I ask.

"Chris told me."

"How did she find out?"

"You know my friend Andrew's ex-wife?"

"The woman who streaked across the football field and got arrested a few years ago?"

"Yeah, well now she's in prison. Drugs—obviously. Anyway, she's in the *same* prison as Rowan. Word is, she heard about the baby from someone who visited her."

I am very aware of the intensity in Emma's eyes. I sigh and drag my fingers through my hair. Truth is, I'm relieved. And, also, I feel bad for Rowan. It's clear the woman is extremely mentally unstable—considering she killed three women—and I'm sure this news only exacerbates her condition.

"How did she take it, do you know?"

Emma shakes her head. "Nope, Chris just told me that she found out and that's literally all I know."

I take another deep breath and lean back in my chair.

"Well, it doesn't really matter now, does it? Nothing she can do about it now."

FIFTY-SIX

KELLAN

From: BanjoForever_RV@jjmail.com
To: PalmerK1982@jjmail.com
Subject: Tree

Kellan,

Please go to our old spot at The Cliff. Do you remember which tree was my favorite? I called her Laverne? She's the one on your right, as you're facing the cliff.

Buried on the north side, between two roots, is a metal box. The combination is your birthday.

Open it and then come see me.

I've finally decided to fight.

I love you.
Rowan

FIFTY-SEVEN

KELLAN

My heart hammers as I stare down at the corner of the silver metal box. I toss the shovel to the side and drop to my knees. Rain runs down my face, pouring off the tip of my nose as I use my hands to brush away the rest of the mud.

Finally, I'm able to unwedge the box from the roots. A combination lock secures the top from the bottom.

I push up to stand, cradle the box under my arm and jog to my truck so that whatever is in it, won't get wet.

I slide behind the wheel and shut and lock the door.

After wiping away the remaining dirt with the sleeve of my shirt, I spin the lock, using my birthday as the code.

My hands tremble as I open the box.

On top is an envelope. In it, a handful of letters, hand-written by Rowan.

FIFTY-EIGHT

LETTER ONE

When I began my criminal investigator training, I'll never forget, one day, while reviewing one of my written tests, the instructor told me to, quote, "always cover your ass." In other words, never leave anything open for interpretation.

I think that's why I'm writing these letters.

I think because something in my gut tells me I might need them one day.

So, Kellan, on that note, here I go ...

It was on our wedding anniversary, of all days, when I told Shepherd about Alyssa Kaing, Macy Swift, and Cora Granger. I don't even remember how it came up, or why I told him in the first place. We'd celebrated our anniversary at home with pizza and cheap champagne, our favorite way to celebrate anything. We'd both had a lot to drink and were on the back porch reminiscing on the past, which always leads to dark conversation.

I told him everything my therapist, Amber, had confided in me a week earlier after inviting me out for coffee, where she confessed her client's worst transgressions in hopes I'd be able to do something about them. I told Shepherd that Alyssa Kaing had confessed to witnessing child abuse but did nothing to stop it, that Macy Swift was swindling money from her sick-kid charity, and that Cora Granger was a social worker who'd been fired for complete incompetence resulting in child negligence.

It sickened him.

He asked what I, the town detective, was going to do about it. I explained to him that I couldn't just go and arrest these people without proper evidence.

After what seemed like an eternity of silence, he looked at me, the moon twinkling in his dark eyes.

He said: "You can't do anything without proper evidence, huh? That's what everyone said about us, you know? Think of all the people who could have stepped in and saved us before we were broken, and didn't because of goddamn red tape."

And then he said something that I'll never forget:

"Those children's blood is on your hands, Rowan, by not doing anything."

FIFTY-NINE
LETTER TWO

The days surrounding Shepherd losing his job were dark. Very dark. Ever since Shepherd was diagnosed with borderline personality disorder at age fifteen, I have been very careful to keep his life as steady and calm as possible. Change is bad. Change is something that can spin him into an episode almost instantly.

Shepherd's childhood was much worse than mine. While I was simply cast aside, Shepherd was sexually abused by his father, who, it was later revealed had sexually abused three other children before he was finally convicted. This is when Shepherd was put into the system and treated like every other child who passed through the doors.

But Shepherd was different.

It wasn't until an FBI special agent, a woman named Darla Thatcher, demanded that Shepherd have full psychiatric testing after having interviewed him several times and established a friendship with him, that his serious mental illness came to light.

Back then, Shepherd went by his first name, Randall. He was called RS, short for Randall Shepherd Velky. I believe that is how Agent Darla Thatcher referred to him.

To this day, Shepherd still talks about Darla. How she was the only person, aside from me, that truly cared for him. The only person to not give up on him.

The only person he trusted.

They kept in touch, Darla and Shepherd, through email, until the day she passed away of breast cancer.

The day after, Shepherd was laid off from work.

SIXTY

LETTER THREE

I found Shepherd's pills in the trashcan. The bottle was almost completely full, which meant he hadn't been taking them for weeks, if not longer. When I confronted him about it, and asked why he'd stopped taking them, he said: "I don't like the way they make me feel."

I told him this was not acceptable, an argument ensued, which spun into him asking me if I was having an affair.

I said no.

Do you want to know the really messed up thing? My first thought at that moment wasn't shame, or how my husband knew that I had romantic feelings for my coworker, but instead, it was worry that he might know that the other man in my life is you. I didn't want you to lose your job. I couldn't do that to you, the man I truly loved.

Shepherd said he'd looked at my cell phone records earlier that week and noticed dozens of calls and texts in the middle of the night.

I told him I was texting with Amber. (Her name was the only one I could come up with, probably because I'd had an appointment with her earlier that day.)

Shepherd rolled his eyes at this, not believing I was texting with my therapist in the middle of the night. I redirected the conversation to his pills, and demanded he begin taking them again.

After leaving the room, I watched from the doorway as Shepherd plucked the pills from the arm rest, hurled them against the wall, then hit himself in the head over and over.

This was right after Alyssa Kaing was murdered.

SIXTY-ONE

LETTER FOUR

You know that feeling you get before a bad thunderstorm? That weird, ominous feeling of doom deep in your gut? That's what I felt the day Alyssa Kaing was killed. I knew something was going to happen that day.

Something bad.

It was just past midnight. I'm sure he thought I was asleep in our bedroom. I wasn't. I couldn't sleep that night. I was too worried about him. I couldn't understand why he'd stopped taking his pills.

Shepherd's mental health journey has been long and exhaustive. The anti-psychotic he'd first been prescribed made him feel lightheaded and confused. He hated it. The doctor reminded us that most patients have to go through several dose adjustments and sometimes, several different medications, to find the right one for their body.

Shepherd once told me that the only reason he took medicine at all was because I was there to remind him to do it. Because I'd threatened to leave him if he didn't.

Because he loved me.

Living with someone with severe mental illness is a day-to-

day journey. It's not something that a pill magically fixes and then you both go on with your life. It's quite the opposite. Dosing needs to be continually adjusted as the patient's body changes or becomes accustomed to it. Physical changes, such as puberty or illness, or any significant life event such as moving, death, marriage, child, can trigger symptoms in which you have to supplement with other medication.

It is constant.

But so was I.

I became obsessed with Shepherd's mental health journey. Or maybe I should say, obsessed with keeping him alive. After all, I'd be dead without him.

I kept multiple folders, tabbed, containing symptom trackers, medication information (and how each affected him), as well as a journal of "bad days" and "good days."

Because of my commitment to ensuring Shepherd followed all necessary medical protocols, he had never fully stopped taking his medication.

Until now. I believe the loss of his job, the loss of his dear friend, and the suspicion that I was cheating on him pushed him over the edge. But I'd promised myself I'd catch him on the other side.

Careful to stay a safe distance behind, I followed Shepherd across town—he in his truck, me in the Explorer. My headlights were off, my head on a swivel, my heart pounding. He'd followed the speed limit through town, then turned onto a side road that skirts Mirror Lake, the lake next to Mirror Lakes neighborhood. I thought I'd lost him until I spotted two taillights a split second before they'd gone dark.

It was a full moon that night, just bright enough to see without using headlights or a flashlight.

Shepherd had parked at a secluded, overgrown launch point along the lakeshore that only locals knew about. Rarely ever used, and no security cameras. I know it well because years ago, he and I had used the point to kayak.

I parked in the ditch a safe distance behind his vehicle, killed the lights, grabbed my keys and slipped out of the SUV, quietly latching the door closed.

The dry, frigid air felt like knives in my lungs as I took off, jogging nimbly over the dirt road in the direction of his truck, having no idea what to expect—or what to say—once I got there.

Shepherd's truck was empty, and he was nowhere in sight.

After shining my phone light around the cab of his truck—what was I looking for? Blood? Him, dead? Someone else, dead? —I spun around, frantically searching the surrounding area, trying to understand what the hell my husband was doing at this time of night. My eyes locked on house lights twinkling through the trees in the distance. The Mirror Lakes subdivision.

I slipped into the trees, quickly finding tracks—bent grass and popped twigs—which verified I was on the right path.

My heart was roaring by the time I reached the manicured back yards of the fancy homes.

I spotted Shepherd just as I emerged from the tree line. His tall, dark silhouette jogged along the shoreline. The moonlight reflected off a white baseball cap, and white dress shirt with a blue collar. I recognized it immediately as the uniform he used to wear when he did door to door sales for the window company, before getting promoted to project manager.

A uniform inspires trust...

He passed home, after home, after home, until slowing at the last house in the neighborhood—Zach and Alyssa Kaing's home. The home of the woman who I'd been told had turned a blind eye to child abuse. I recognized it as the Kaing home instantly from all the gossip surrounding the newcomers who'd built "a castle" in our small town.

Shepherd pivoted, then began hiking up the short hill to the back yard of the home.

I lost him in the shadows for a moment, then he reappeared climbing the back fence that led to the Kaing's property. I remember being shocked at how quickly and easily he scaled the tall fence. Adrenaline, I know now.

At that point I took off sprinting down the shoreline. My arms and legs were tingling, my pulse pounding. I think I knew at that point, deep in my gut, what he was doing.

I struggled to pull myself up the fence. Just as I reached the top, I saw Shepherd slip through the back door of the home. The home was unlocked.

There, clinging onto the top of the fence, I froze. Completely seized up. Paralyzed in inaction. Everything I'd been trained to do as a member of law enforcement suddenly vanished from my brain.

This was not a routine home invasion—it was my husband.

Then, a hair-raising scream as ice-cold as the wind cut through the air.

Like being jolted by electric shock, I snapped out of my trance. I went into protect mode—into fix mode. The thought of calling for backup didn't even enter my mind—not even for a split second. My only thoughts were: protect him; fix it.

I dropped from the fence, spun around, and hid in the trees. There, I waited for him to leave.

Then, I kneeled next to his boot prints in the dirt. As I covered up my husband's tracks, all I could think about was the time, so long ago, that he saved my life.

It was time to repay that debt.

SIXTY-TWO

KELLAN

My eyes lock on Rowan's the second I step into the visitation room.

The corrections officer—a new one, I think, a young kid I've never seen here before—escorts me to the visitation booth where Rowan sits behind a thick pane of glass.

"Fifteen minutes," the kid says, gesturing to the phone mounted on a slab of sheetrock that serves as a divider between this booth and the next. There is very little privacy in prison.

I wait to pick up the phone until the officer returns to his post. Rowan picks up hers.

My heart pounds as I take her in. Every visit, I'm terrified of what I might see. Watching Rowan transform over the months has been nothing short of heart breaking. In the beginning, she and I would simply sit together, our palms touching through the glass, not a single word spoken between us. Some days we'd cry the entire time. As the weeks went on, however, Rowan's emotion subsided and a detached, hardness took its place. She became alarmingly pale, skinny, her once soft curves replaced with muscle and sharp angles. But the hardest thing to see was the change in her eyes. How they went from bursting with emotion to... nothing. Absolutely nothing. Rowan became dead behind the eyes, stoic, completely robotic.

Until today. Until *this* moment. Even through the smudges on the glass that divides us, I can see the excitement, the sense of urgency in those beautiful brown eyes. Her cheeks are even pink.

She's *alive.*

I speak first because I, too, feel like I am bursting at the seams.

"Why didn't you tell me about this months ago? I knew you didn't do it." I blurt into the phone. "I've been here every week for *four* months. Why didn't you tell me, Rowan?"

"I don't expect you to understand."

"Baby." I flatten my hand against the glass, a rush of emotions sweeping through my body. "I do understand, I do, and I don't care. What we need to focus on now is the next steps. Tell me everything. I followed the instructions in your email and found the box. I just need your okay to meet with your lawyer."

"You have my okay."

I exhale. "Good. Now. Tell me everything—leave nothing out."

"Wait, how's Banjo?"

It's the only question she repeats with every visit.

Although I'm impatient, I pull his latest picture from my shirt pocket and press it against the glass. It's of Banjo fetching a stick from the lake earlier in the week. He's mid-swim and smiling around the stick in his mouth. Every visit, I bring a new picture of him, the first being the day I adopted him from the animal shelter after Shepherd dumped him.

Rowan's eyes light up.

"He's doing great. Getting really, really good at swimming. Honey, we need to talk, please. Now."

Rowan nods, and I slide the picture back into my pocket.

She takes a deep, shaky breath. "Do you remember the story you told me that night at The Cliff? Of your brother, Jack, and the night he died from an alcohol overdose?"

"Yes."

"You said: *If I had intervened, would he still be alive? If I had addressed his mental illness, would he still be alive?* You talked about your loyalty to him and how, with family, nothing should be off-limits. That's how I felt when I realized what Shepherd was doing. I blamed his mental illness—not him—and I blamed myself for not taking better care of his medication. That loyalty, that guilt, the mental illness, everything, that's why I chose to help my husband. I was brainwashed, I realize that now, and again, I don't expect you to understand."

I'd figured as much. "I understand," I say simply.

"Thank you. You're the only person who truly would." She takes another deep breath. "When I learned Shepherd was cheating on me with Amber, and then the cops showed up, and I also realized he was going to let me to take the fall for killing those women... the betrayal was so deep, Kellan—I can't even put into words how hurt I was. There was no going back. I wanted to die, right then and there. I didn't care anymore. It's like I totally shut off. Prison here, prison there, it didn't matter. There was no life for me anymore. The man I spent my life caring for, the man I'd put my life on the line for, lied and told the feds that he knew nothing. He allowed me to be convicted for murders he committed. Can you even fathom that kind of betrayal?"

I swipe a tear from my cheek. With Rowan, there is no controlling my emotions, and I don't even care.

"When you told me they had my DNA, I knew that no matter what I said, I was going to be convicted. I pleaded guilty knowing I'd get at least ten years off my sentence and maybe someday I'd even be released early."

Her face hardens. She takes a moment to speak again.

"But then I found out that Shepherd and Amber were having a baby—a *baby*." She swallows deeply. "I... I want you to know that I'm not mad that you didn't tell me, but I wish you had."

"I'm sorry, Rowan. I only found out a few weeks ago. I understand, but please understand my perspective: what good would it have done to tell you at this point?"

"I understand."

"Okay, keep going, we have nine minutes."

"Okay, so when I found out about the baby, I... I couldn't bear the thought of a child being born into his care. I couldn't bear the thought of a child growing up with Shepherd, a serial killer, as their father. It starts the cycle all over again, do you know what I mean? Aunt Jenny..." A knot catches her throat. Her eyes fill with tears. Her aunt's recent passing has been hard on her. "Aunt Jenny once told me that someone has to stand up and break the cycle—and I'm going to do that right now. I'm going to ensure Shepherd can't hurt anyone ever again. That child needs a chance, and I'm going to give it to them."

"Good, Rowan." More tears. "Okay, let me go through the items that were in the box, and make sure I have everything, before we blow this thing up." I pull a crumpled piece of paper from my pocket, damp from sweat. I begin counting off the items with my finger. "In the box was: Handwritten letters from you—a confession of sorts—including the day you told Shepherd about Alyssa, Macy, and Cora, and ending with a detailed outline of everything you did to protect your husband after you realized what he was doing. Also included is your detailed assessment on how he got away with everything, including how he visited the women wearing his old uniform from when he did window sales, inspiring trust, before later killing them. The women recognized him, and therefore didn't initially attack him, giving him the few seconds he needed to disable them.

"Two, a copy of Shepherd's medical records, including his psychiatric assessment as well as the late Special Agent Darla Thatcher's assessment, who worked with him when he was a child.

"Three, a burner cell phone which contains videos you took while following him. These videos show Shepherd approaching Macy Swift at the trail the night she was murdered, another shows him sneaking into Cora Granger's home the night she was murdered, and then there are videos of him leaving both scenes.

"Four, a thumb drive containing twenty-seven photos you took of the physical tracks at each crime scene before covering them up.

"Five, a tracker that you put on his truck, after he'd stopped taking his pills and you'd become worried about his mental state. This tracker pins him to the location of the last two murders, at the time and date of each.

"Lastly, the hard drive of your basement computer which shows that Shepherd researched the three women extensively before each were killed, as well as endless extremely disturbing searches about torture and murder. That's it, right?"

Rowan nods.

We stare at each other, both momentarily overwhelmed by the weight of the moment and what will come of this.

A tear rolls down her face and I want so badly to reach through the screen and pull her into my arms. The woman I have been unable to let go of, even after she was convicted of murder. The woman who I knew, deep in my soul, was innocent. The woman who I am so deeply, madly, insanely in love with.

"I feel awful that I allowed everything to spin out of control, that I lied to you, to everyone, that I—

"No," I interrupt. "Rowan, from this day forward, we put

one foot in front of the other and leave the past in rearview mirror. Only forward movement. Deal?"

She wipes the tear from her cheek and the sweetest softest smile crosses her face. "Deal."

SIXTY-THREE

AMBER

"You have *got* to stop hyperventilating, Amber. You are going to hurt the baby."

"*Hurt* the baby? *This* baby?" I jab a finger into my protruding stomach. "This is the baby of a fucking serial killer, Emma!"

Emma shakes her head and sits on the couch, no longer affected by my emotional outbursts. I, on the other hand, continue to pace the living room like a rabid, caged animal—the living room of the home that Shepherd and I moved into just *four* days ago. The mortgage I now share with a serial killer.

The second after the FBI showed up at our door and took Shepherd away in handcuffs, I called Emma, absolutely hysterical. She pulled into the driveway four hours later.

"Amber, you need someone here after I leave, to take care of you and Connor."

Connor is sitting at the kitchen table, playing on his stupid device. My eyes fill with tears.

"Please call someone," she urges. "Call Mark."

I snort. "Mark has already submitted an emergency request for full custody of Connor. He can fuck himself. I'm not calling

him and I don't want anyone else here." I look at the clock.
"What time are you leaving?"

"At six-thirty, so, forty-five minutes from now."

"I'll be fine."

"I really think—"

"*Shh,*" I hiss. "Turn it up—the television!" I point to Shepherd's face on the screen.

Emma grabs the remote and turns up the evening news show currently airing.

"In a plot twist usually reserved for Hollywood movies, Shepherd Velky, the husband of infamous Detective Rowan Velky, who was convicted of three counts of first-degree murder, has been arrested in connection to those same murders.

Rowan Velky has served months in prison for the murders of Alyssa Kaing, Macy Swift, and Cora Granger. However, the recent discovery of new evidence has revealed that her husband, Shepherd, was the real killer. Our sources tell us that in an effort to protect her mentally ill husband, Ms. Velky concealed evidence that would implicate her husband, and then sacrificed herself in his place. As if that's not enough, rumors are, Shepherd was secretly having an affair with Ms. Velky's therapist while all of this was going on. Rowan Velky was quietly released from prison four days before her husband was arrested. Though Ms. Velky was charged with several crimes including tampering with evidence and falsifying reports, she was able to strike a deal with the judge and count her time already served as payment for the charges. Velky's whereabouts are unknown at this time, but here's to hoping she's drinking a margarita on a beach somewhere far, far away..."

I spin around, my heart feeling like it is about to burst out of my chest. "They're going to arrest me as an accomplice, Emma, I know it. I'm next."

"No, they're not. You didn't know Shepherd was killing those women."

"They'll find something to pin me with, I know it. The whole country knows I was his mistress while he was murdering all those women—God I can't believe I was so, *so* stupid." I sink onto the couch, drop my head into my hands, and begin sobbing. "Everyone hates me. They're going to take Connor from me and I'm going to have this devil baby in prison, I know it."

"Stop, Amber. *Stop.*"

"I don't understand where she is," I bellow. "Where is she? Where is Rowan?"

"I don't know. No one knows. They released her secretly to avoid the media. No one knows. Amber." Emma glances out the window. "She's not going to come for you. You've got to let that go."

"I was fucking her husband while she was spilling her guts to me on my couch. I was her *therapist*, Emma, and also the person who went to the cops and told them she killed those women. And now I am pregnant with her soon-to-be ex-husband's baby. You really think she doesn't want revenge?"

"She's not going to hurt you." Emma grabs my chin and turns my face to hers. "You *have* to relax."

I shake my head. I can't even respond. I am spinning. I feel like I am about to internally combust. My entire world has been flipped upside down.

Unable to sit any longer, I walk to the window and peek through the curtains. Thankfully, the media van that had been parked outside all day is gone.

"Come in the kitchen," Emma stands, "let's make some tea."

It's four hours later, an unseasonably cool night.

Emma is gone, Connor is asleep, and I am staring out the window.

A leaf falls from a tree, slowly flittering back and forth on the wind.

I watch it, wishing I were as free at that leaf.

And that's when I see her.

Rowan Velky's dark silhouette emerging from the tree line.

SIXTY-FOUR

SPECIAL AGENT BRIAN BRIGGS

I've interviewed my fair share of mentally disturbed suspects, but Shepherd Velky takes the cake. It was clear from the moment we arrested him that he was a very unwell man. Our interviews have been broken up between psychiatric and medical evaluations. As the lead agent on the case, it's been rather frustrating. Anti-psychotic medication was administered almost immediately, which has been an unexpected hurdle for our conversations, as doses are continually being adjusted.

His lawyer has already plead insanity, and in this case, I believe it is warranted. Mr. Velky will spend the rest of his life locked in a psychiatric hospital, where he belongs.

I study him, sitting across from me in an orange jumpsuit, wrists and ankles shackled. He stares back at me, vacant, blood-shot eyes. Eerily still and calm. Just like when he admitted to the murders. There is no remorse in the man, no shame, no regret. Shepherd Velky had a mission, one that he has now completed.

Agent Zeal is standing behind me. An armed guard hovers in the corner, and another outside the door. Outside the parking lot is packed with media.

"Mr. Velky, in our last interview, we spoke about your father. Your childhood, specifically, and the abuse you encountered. I'd like to return to that subject, if that's okay with you."

"Yes."

"Thank you. During your medical evaluation, the doctor noted countless small scars all over your body. Each one about one inch in length. Can you talk to me about that?"

"It was part of my punishment." His voice is low, dull. Deadened. "Among other punishments, my father would cut me every time I acted out of line."

"I'm sorry to hear that. Is this why you mutilated the bodies of Aylssa Kaing, Macy Swift, and Cora Granger with the letter X?"

"Yes. They deserved to be punished, and their sins deserved to be revealed to the world."

"Why?"

"It was time."

"I understand you had a rough couple of months leading up to you murdering Alyssa Kaing. Is this what you're referring to?"

"Not really. Everything that happened were signs that it was time."

"Time for what?"

"A change."

"What do you mean, a change?"

"A change in the status quo. In the never-ending cycle of abuse."

"And killing the women allowed for that change?"

"Yes."

"Why didn't you leave that up to us?"

"My entire childhood was left up to you and look what happened."

SIXTY-FIVE

ROWAN

Listen. I know you think I hurt Amber. Okay, maybe not hurt her, but at least got my revenge.

I didn't.

I'm not going to lie. I thought about it. But, the truth is, I've decided that the internal turmoil Amber is experiencing now—and will for the rest of her life—is punishment enough. After all, what goes around always comes back around, doesn't it? In Amber's case, it's come back around in her forever-title of mistress of a murderer, and also in her child of a serial killer.

So instead, I snuck over to Amber's house in the middle of the night—to avoid being spotted by the media—to forgive her. To get *my* closure, to take the first step in letting everything go. When you forgive, you heal. I read that quote while in prison. It resonated with me.

I want to heal and I want to start over.

Today is day one of starting over.

Kellan reaches over and lays his hand over mine. Smiling, I thread my fingers through his, and with my other hand, trace the veins on the back of his hand. He has such manly, sexy hands.

"We're boarding."

Little butterflies tickle my stomach. The same ones that awaken every time he looks at me in that way... which, really, is every time.

I glance down at the text on my phone showing a picture of Banjo, sprawled out on an expensive leather couch, asleep, tongue lolling.

Kellan grins. "We might never get that dog back."

I type a response.

> Me: Thanks, again, Chris. For everything, and for watching Banjo for us. And please tell Emma we said hi. Keep me updated on my buddy. We're boarding.

I slide my phone into my pocket and take a deep breath. "Let's do this."

Kellan and I stand together, and hand in hand, step onto the jet bridge.

"Now boarding first class, Delta flight 5264, to Paris, France ..."

A LETTER FROM THE AUTHOR

Dear Readers – let's stay in touch! 🖤

Click here to hear about my new releases with Storm:

www.stormpublishing.co/amanda-mckinney

Click here to be included in my personal newsletter:

www.amandamckinneyauthor.com/contact

If you enjoyed *A Marriage of Lies* and could spare a few moments to leave a review that would be hugely appreciated. Even a short review can make all the difference in encouraging a reader to discover my books for the first time. Thank you so much!

facebook.com/AmandaMcKinneyAuthor

instagram.com/amandamckinneyauthor

tiktok.com/amandamckinneyauthor

Made in United States
North Haven, CT
11 June 2024

53470443R00161